"We shoul... ...id, pulling h...

Juliette licked the raindrops off her lips. "We should...but then I'd never get over my fear of storms. But if we were to replace the bad memories with something wonderful..."

Doug groaned, conceding defeat. He wanted, *needed* this woman. He intended to take it slowly, but once he covered her mouth with his and tasted the erotic mixture of rainwater and Juliette, he was lost. Unable to stop himself, he ran his hands down her body, skimming her breasts, touching her intimately.

Juliette let out a whimper of assent, a soft mew of satisfaction. Doug was amazed at how responsive Juliette was to his touch. And just when he thought he'd been granted his deepest desire, she shifted her stance, giving him greater access. He'd wanted her permission, he'd received her submission instead. The feelings she inspired in him should have sent him running, but he was beyond reason. Beyond anything except this woman and this moment.

Juliette's body tensed, letting Doug know he'd brought her to the brink. Bracing her against the door for support, he gave her what she craved. "Juliette," he rasped in her ear. "What are you going to think about next time it rains?"

"You," she said, as her body exploded.

Dear Reader,

A secret fantasy. Don't we all wish we had the nerve to make our fantasies come to life? Welcome to the second of four lush island resorts dedicated to making your most personal fantasies come true. Come meet Juliette Stanton, a senator's daughter and Chicago's infamous runaway bride. Only she knows why she fled the altar, but she isn't talking to anyone, especially the press. The island of Secret Fantasy is the perfect retreat to regroup and discover what she wants out of life, while indulging in erotic fantasies with a handsome stranger. Little does she realize that her sexy stranger is a reporter! Doug Houston arrives wanting Juliette's story and leaves wanting Juliette herself! But will his secrets destroy any chance they have of being together?

The FANTASIES INC. miniseries is very special to me. With all four stories, readers are in for a Seductive, Secret, Intimate and Wild ride. Enjoy! I hope I'm making your reading fantasies come true. You can write to me at: P.O. Box 483, Purchase, NY 10577. Or check out my Web site at www.carlyphillips.com.

Happy reading,

Carly Phillips

P.S. Be sure to watch for my first book in Harlequin's newest—and hottest—series: Blaze! *Body Heat*, the second book in the SEXY CITY NIGHTS miniseries will heat up the bookstores in September 2001. Don't miss it.

SECRET FANTASY
Carly Phillips

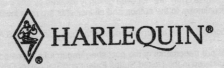

HARLEQUIN®

TORONTO • NEW YORK • LONDON
AMSTERDAM • PARIS • SYDNEY • HAMBURG
STOCKHOLM • ATHENS • TOKYO • MILAN • MADRID
PRAGUE • WARSAW • BUDAPEST • AUCKLAND

This book is dedicated to the people who make my professional fantasies come true. To Birgit Davis-Todd and Brenda Chin, for making me a part of the Temptation family. And to Maureen Walters, for having the vision to take a chance on me. Thank you all for your constant faith and support.

ISBN 0-373-25936-0

SECRET FANTASY

Copyright © 2001 by Karen Drogin.

_____Prologue_____

MERRILEE SCHAEFER-WESTON flipped through the freshly delivered paperwork on her desk. The file in her hand held detailed information on Juliette Stanton—her likes, dislikes, dress size and even shoe size. Everything and anything necessary to prepare and make a woman's fantasy come true. Juliette Stanton, otherwise known as Chicago's Runaway Bride, was an unwilling public figure thanks to the scandal surrounding her aborted wedding and her illustrious senator father's reputation. Now she was a client of Fantasies, Inc.

Merrilee read the first question she posed to all clients, though she knew the words by heart. _What is your fantasy?_

The answer always proved to be elusive. In Juliette Stanton's case: _To experience the luxury of being catered to and doted upon by a very special man. To feel desirable, be the center of his universe and forget the hurt of a broken engagement._

Now _this_ was what Fantasies, Inc. was all about. Merrilee's four lush island resorts were founded for the express purpose of making people's dreams, wishes and longings come true. And though she could give Juliette only what she sought, Merrilee always tried to go that one step further, by giving her guests a happier ending than she, herself, had had.

A knock sounded at the door, calling her attention. She rose, expecting her ten o'clock appointment. "Come in."

The door opened and a tall, imposing-looking man entered the room. "Mr. Houston?" At his nod, she gestured for him to enter. "I'm Merrilee Schaefer-Weston. Welcome to Secret Fantasy. I hope you had a good flight?"

He settled himself in the chair in front of her desk. "Perfect. Call me Doug, please." He treated her to a charming grin that no doubt worked wonders on any eligible, breathing younger woman.

She braced her hands on the desk and got to the point. "I assume you have a fantasy you want fulfilled?"

"Doesn't everybody?"

"Thanks to this business I've discovered that to be true."

Though he laughed, Merrilee recognized his reluctance to talk. "Would you prefer to tour the island before revealing your fantasy?"

He shook his head and shifted uncomfortably in his seat. "I'm a reporter for the *Chicago Tribune*."

Interesting, Merrilee thought. And as she looked into his eyes, she realized his discomfort was real. "Go on, please."

He cleared his throat. "I'm coming off a relationship that ended badly. I was involved with a woman for the last two years but I wasn't ready to commit. I didn't tell her that though." He ran a hand through his black hair. "Still, I thought things were going well—but appearances can be deceiving."

"And relationships can be messy and sometimes unpleasant."

"You understand."

She nodded. More than he knew. She glanced at the thin band of gold and rubies encircling the third finger on her right hand—a symbol of the love she'd had too briefly and lost as a result of the Vietnam War. Her life hadn't gone as planned, but then whose did? Fate generally took over. "How does your recent past relate to your present desire?" she asked Doug.

"My ex and I shared business and pleasure. We had fun and because she was well-connected in certain social circles, I trusted her information." He shook his head, his frustration obvious.

"I take it she wasn't reliable?"

"She was reliable until she asked outright when I'd be ready to get married. I wasn't. But she seemed to accept it well, or so I thought. But she decided I was using her and fed me information that, inexplicably, I could no longer confirm once my story ran." His lips twisted in a wry grin. "The typical woman scorned."

"And were you? Using her, I mean?"

He paused, giving her question thought. That he didn't answer her with an outright "no" told Merrilee he valued truth as much as she did.

He let out a groan. "At the time I would have said no. But looking back, I suppose half the thrill of the relationship was the personal—as opposed to professional—'in' she gave me to certain social circles and people I wanted to expose."

She appreciated his honesty and nodded in empathy. "And now you're here. So tell me—what is your fantasy?"

He leaned forward in his seat. "To make up for what I've done. I need to be able to look at myself in the mirror." He drew a deep breath. "I need to know I can put a woman before myself."

"So you're asking me to…"

"Pair me up with Juliette Stanton, Chicago's Runaway Bride. I know she's booked to come down here."

Merrilee narrowed her gaze. "And you know this how?" Because if he'd gone to the trouble to hunt Juliette down and discover information other reporters hadn't, his agenda would bring Merrilee as well as Juliette Stanton nothing but trouble.

"A tip from someone who felt I needed to know. Look, that story I just mentioned? It involved Juliette Stanton's fiancé. And I have a hard time believing her run from the altar was coincidence. The gossip rags are holding her up for ridicule and the radio stations are running contests about why she ran. My gut tells me the woman's hurting and I'm the cause. I want to help her get past it."

"And what of your journalistic instincts? How do I know you aren't looking to expose her story like the rest of the reporters out there? How do I know you won't use the information *should* it fall into your lap?" Merrilee's business and reputation, and Juliette's well-being, hinged on his answer and his sincerity.

She held his gaze, making sure she didn't miss anything, from a tic in his jaw to a flash of guilt in his eyes. But all she discovered was his ability to look her head-on.

He raised his shoulders in a shrug. "You don't. Any man you fix her up with can conceivably find out the same information and use it against her whether he's a reporter or not."

Merrilee nodded. He had a point. Anyone could potentially uncover the reasons Juliette had run from the altar and expose them for money or personal gain—something Juliette, the senator's daughter and runaway bride had to know going into her fantasy. She hadn't put any restrictions or limitations on who or what kind of man she wanted to fulfill her needs. Merrilee inclined her head and waited for him to continue.

He didn't disappoint her. "Look, I'm here, I'm spilling my guts and I'm giving you my word—I'm not looking to hurt her. That's the best I can do."

Merrilee nodded slowly. "Tell me something, Doug. Do you believe in happily ever after?" Merrilee needed to know more about Doug Houston's character and intentions before she agreed to any match.

His eyebrows crinkled and his jaw clenched tight,

then he let out a loud breath of air. "Yes, ma'am, I do. My parents are celebrating their fortieth anniversary this year."

"That's wonderful, but evasive. Not that I'm surprised, since you're a reporter. But do you believe in happily ever after for *you?*"

"*If* I found the right woman, and *if* she could put up with me, then yes, I do." His blue-eyed stare never wavered, then obviously satisfied he'd made his point, he stood. "I won't take any more of your time but I'd appreciate it if you'd think about my request and get back to me."

"I'll do that." Merrilee rose and shook Doug's hand before letting him go. He shut the door behind him.

She clasped her hands in front of her, on top of Juliette Stanton's file, and paused in thought. Merrilee had been in this business a long time and based her decisions on experience, instinct and faith. She could deny Doug Houston his request, a risk he'd taken laying all his cards on the table. Or she could let fate take over.

Juliette needed to heal. Doug needed to atone for his mistakes. *If* Merrilee gave in to his request, while making Juliette Stanton feel cherished and special, Doug could discover he was a human being beneath the reporter exterior. He could realize that people were more important than a career.

And love was the most important thing of all.

1

"FIX YOUR SKIRT. It's tucked under at the hem."

Juliette Stanton sighed and shook out the ruffled bottom of the denim miniskirt she'd borrowed from her freer, more eclectic sister, and adjusted the loose flowing cotton top hanging off one shoulder. "This is insanity at its finest." She zipped her suitcase closed and turned back to face Gillian, her twin. "Tell me again why you spent your hard-earned savings so I could take a vacation." Juliette loved her sister dearly but didn't want her worrying or pampering her just because she was going through a difficult time.

Juliette slipped the luggage tag into the compartment on the side of the suitcase, muttering as she packed and not giving Gillian a chance to answer. "Much as I appreciate the gesture, I don't want a vacation. I don't need a vacation. I simply need to get back into my life."

Gillian laughed. "Exactly right. You need to get a life, which is why you're going on this trip." She placed her hands on her hips, wrinkling the cream-colored pantsuit she'd borrowed from Juliette. The twins had traded outfits as part of an elaborate plan to elude the reporters and get Juliette to the airport unnoticed.

Though Juliette understood the need for the charade, she hated the deceit. She shot her sister a disgruntled look. "I'm going on this trip because you cared enough to arrange it for me," she said, her voice softening.

"And you have to admit, getting away from the tabloids and rumor mill has to hold a certain appeal," Gillian added.

Knowing her sister was right, Juliette reached over and squeezed her tightly.

"You know I love you, too," her sister said.

Juliette knew. If not for her twin's solid support, getting through these past few weeks would have been impossible. Since the day Juliette had bolted from the church, the reporters had been ruthless, staking out both Juliette's house and Gillian's apartment in hopes of getting the scoop on the Runaway Bride. But no one outside of Gillian or the groom knew why Juliette had called off the wedding.

And no one would. At least not until she figured out how to protect her father and let him retire from the senate, his reputation and pride intact. At which point the press could have at Stuart Barnes and his shady dealings.

"So have you heard from the louse?" Gillian grabbed a pillow and sat down.

Juliette shook her head, emotion clogging her throat. Although she'd never say she'd been *in* love with Stuart, what they'd shared had been comfortable and secure. Too comfortable, she acknowledged now.

With hindsight she could see the reasons for her engagement. They were twofold and simple. Juliette adored her mother and father and idolized their loving relationship. They were wonderful parents who'd managed to keep a family intact despite the fishbowl in which they lived. Juliette wanted a stable family and comfortable marriage like her parents had. She'd believed she could share those things with Stuart, a childhood friend she thought she knew well.

And then there was the *other* reason she'd gotten engaged—the one Juliette hated to admit, even to herself. While neither her mother nor her father had ever asked for her to sacrifice, she'd always taken the expected road. Perhaps because Gillian had taken on the part of the wild child, Juliette, the older sister by a matter of minutes, had always seen her role as that of the good girl. So when Stuart set his sights on Juliette, she'd fallen into the relationship without question. Because she'd recently been hurt by a man more interested in her father's name and connections than in her, Stuart who'd always been a part of her life, seemed safe. And because her parents liked and trusted him, they'd been thrilled and could claim "they knew Juliette and Stuart belonged together all along."

But they hadn't belonged together and if Juliette had looked hard enough, she'd have seen the signs.

Yet she'd never questioned their relationship, not even their lukewarm sex life, which deep down she'd blamed herself for. Certainly her previous painful affair hadn't boosted her confidence. Perhaps she'd known all along that if she questioned her decision, she'd discover she'd repeated her mistake. Stuart wanted leverage in achieving her father's soon-to-be-vacant senate seat. Nothing more. Especially not Juliette Stanton, the woman.

"Earth to Juliette." Gillian snapped her fingers.

She shook her head. "Sorry. Too much thinking going on. No, I haven't heard a word since our confrontation in the church. But what's he going to say? 'Thanks for keeping the press off my back so I can take your father's place in November'?"

Gillian sniffed in disdain. "He could say, 'I'm an ass.' That would be a start."

"I agree. And considering he all but threatened to drag Dad down with him, he's trusting me to keep quiet about why I bolted." Stuart was her father's protégé. His choice to succeed him. If Stuart's shady dealings came to light, Juliette's father, his decisions and choices would all be suspect, tainting the good he'd accomplished during his tenure.

Gillian clenched her teeth. "He's trusting your love for Dad."

Juliette let out a harsh laugh. "He's certainly not banking on my love for him." Or what was left of it.

She'd thought they shared caring and consideration based on their years of friendship. Even after scandal had hit the papers, accusing Stuart's business partner, Congressman Haywood, of laundering Mob money through Coffee Connections, their import-export business, she'd believed her fiancé's denials. In this instance, she hadn't shut her eyes to the truth, rather, like her father, she'd believed in Stuart's integrity. And since Stuart hadn't been labeled as an accessory and the story about Congressman Haywood had later been retracted, she'd trusted her instincts.

How wrong she'd been. Again. She'd caught Stuart red-handed, his business partner and the reputed Mob boss having a tête-à-tête in the church minutes before she and Stuart were to be married.

She faced her life and the lies at last, confronted him and walked out. And though her parents supported her decision and her need for privacy, she knew they too were waiting for an explanation.

Gillian let out a groan. "We both agree that this needs to be kept under wraps until you figure out a plan, but I don't like the fact that Stuart's let the press pin you with the Runaway Bride rap." She picked up a videotape box containing the movie of the same name. "You might have similar hair—did I mention I *love* the curls?" She flicked at one of Juliette's long spirals with her fingers. "And since this is the last time I have to sit for hours with the blow-dryer to copy your stick-straight hair to fake out those reporters, I'm eternally grateful."

Juliette laughed. "Thanks." She loved her new look, too.

She'd secretly always envied her sister's ability to thumb her nose at convention and just be herself, cameras and press be damned. Juliette hoped her new loose-flowing perm, like her free-spirited sister's, would change both her appearance and outlook for her upcoming trip. If there was ever a time to let loose, this vacation would have to be it.

"Did you pick up those things for me at the mall?" Juliette asked her twin. If her fiancé had been interested in planning a honeymoon instead of a political campaign and election, she'd have the wardrobe basics ready to go. But Stuart had insisted they couldn't get away. Now she knew why.

"Got 'em. I put them in the empty suitcase while you were on the phone earlier. And you'd be so proud of how I finagled that trip without being followed." Gillian grinned, obviously pleased with herself.

Juliette cringed. "I'm sure I don't want to know. It seems everyone's been making sacrifices to accommodate me these days." She hated the high maintenance perception that was the result of this nightmare. First her stylist had agreed to do spiral curls and a haircut at her house, not wanting his salon inundated by the press, and now her sister was running around like an undercover spy—and loving every minute.

"They're not sacrifices, they're favors. And we love you, so we don't mind. But I hate that you're stuck in the house and practically branded, you know?" Gillian tapped her foot impatiently against the hardwood floor. "Damn, I wish we could leak this story." She shook her head. "But we can't."

"Not yet. Dad's established a long tradition of serving this country. He's well liked and respected. He has a place in history he's *earned*. No way I'll let him go out tainted by scandal. He doesn't deserve it."

Gillian nodded. "I agree."

For their father's sake, the secret had to stay secret a little longer. Juliette drew a deep breath. "I'm ready."

"Okay." Gillian rose from her seat and grabbed for a bag.

"So let me get this plan straight. I drive your car dressed like you, while you sit in the passenger seat pretending to be me," Juliette said.

"So far so good."

"We drive past the reporters, to your apartment where the rest of the vultures are waiting, and pull into the secure underground garage."

Gillian nodded. "Right. Where they have no access." Her laugh bordered on giddy at the thought of outwitting the press. "They think you're visiting me and to reinforce the impression, I, dressed as you, go up to the lobby and out to the convenience store on the corner before heading back inside. They won't be looking for us to go anywhere while we're presumably hanging out together."

"Meanwhile I slip into the back seat of Dad's car,

driven by his chauffeur, cover myself with a blanket and end up at the airport."

"Exactly. And if anyone happens to see you, they'll think you're me. No one's going to bother following me once I have no access to you. Voilà! You're home free and on your way."

Juliette stretched her arms out wide. "Ready to begin a glorious week of fun, sun and solitude."

Her sister's gaze darted from hers. "You got the first two right," she muttered.

Juliette narrowed her eyes. She'd grown up in the shadow of her daring, more adventurous twin and she knew Gillian better than she knew herself. The shifting eyeballs and muttering under her breath meant her sister was up to something. "What aren't you telling me?" Juliette asked.

"Not a blessed thing." Gillian glanced at her watch. "You don't want to miss your flight. We need to get going."

Juliette grabbed her suitcase. "Okay. And if I haven't said it before because I was too busy complaining, I am touched you'd spend your savings on me—and I want to pay you back." Although both girls had trust funds set up in their name from their grandmother's will, neither lived off the interest or principal. Each chose to make their own way in the world, Juliette as a public relations consultant for a pharmaceutical company, Gillian as a teacher.

"It's not a gift if you pay me," her sister reminded her. "Consider this my broken wedding gift to you."

Juliette squeezed her sister's hand. "I'm so lucky to have you."

Gillian grinned. "Yeah, you are."

They made their way into the two-car garage attached to the old cottage Juliette rented, where Gillian had parked her car.

"Promise me something?" Gillian asked. "It's private on the island and if we've done this right, no cameras are following you, no press is around to ask questions. Let loose and be yourself, okay?"

"You read my mind." Juliette wasn't surprised that the twin connection was at work again. She laughed, knowing she'd already decided to take advantage of this time to be free and experiment with who Juliette Stanton really was. She never should have fought Gillian's attempt to get her to take a vacation. She settled herself into the driver's seat, put the key in the ignition and turned her wrist.

"So," she said over the rumble of the car's motor. "Let the adventure begin."

ONE WEEK after his initial visit, Doug Houston stood in the luxurious open-air lobby of Secret Fantasy's main building waiting for the object of his fantasy.

His fantasy.

Guilt swamped him over the thought of this whole damned trip and the charade he'd have to employ to get his story. Guilt wasn't an emotion Doug was familiar with, especially when it came to getting the job done. But this job was too important to let something like unexpected feelings get in the way.

He was at this resort tracking down Juliette Stanton, Chicago's Runaway Bride, so he could dig up dirt on her ex-fiancé. And therein lay the source of his guilt. He could console himself with the fact that he wasn't out to dig up dirt on *her* and in that, at least, he hadn't lied to Merrilee.

But Doug had a nagging feeling the reasons for Juliette's run from the altar had everything to do with Doug's recent troubles—and his journalist father had taught him never to ignore a burning gut. Treat it with antacids, maybe, but pay close attention. After the last fiasco, Doug damn well would.

Doug wasn't green and knew to be on the lookout for an unreliable source. Problem was he'd never thought to distrust so close to home and when his latest story had come crashing down around him he'd been taken off guard. His adopted father, a journalist and a man respected by all, had trained him to be the best. Yet Doug's fall from grace had been swift and as public as his damning headline about Congressman Haywood's meeting with a reputed Mob boss and the laundering of money through a supposed legitimate coffee business.

The congressman was the business partner of Juliette Stanton's fiancé, the man aspiring to her father's senate seat. A man, Doug thought, who was just as corrupt as his partner. Doug still believed his story was true. He just didn't have the proof he needed to back up his story or support his claim. Proof he was certain Juliette Stanton possessed.

Doug ran a hand through his collar-length, wind-blown hair—another part of this charade. No haircut, no shave until after his time on the island was through. After he was certain Senator Stanton's daughter wouldn't recognize him from the more clean-cut picture in his *Tribune* column.

A week on this tropical island wouldn't be a hardship if his father wasn't still in the hospital. Though he'd normally enjoy paradise, Doug had to follow up on this latest tip regarding Juliette and get the hell out. A tip he believed no one else had. And with some serious cash in the right hands he hoped to be the only one who knew Juliette had left town. The only one to spend an uninterrupted week alone with the Runaway Bride—once he got the final okay from Merrilee. She hadn't thrown him off the island when he'd shown up in time to coincide with Juliette's visit, but he knew he was on probation.

He'd paid good money to an old military pal of his father's to dig hard and deep until he broke Merrilee's security system and came up with the information Doug needed—Juliette Stanton's fantasy. And in the process, he'd discovered the woman was hurting and he'd been forced to accept some of the blame.

No matter how he consoled himself with truth—that his fantasy *would* help Juliette Stanton forget her pain, and that he wasn't out to hurt *her*—the fact remained, he was using another woman for information. Again.

Doug had no choice.

This story would reinstate him as the *Tribune's* ace political reporter, a place he wanted desperately to be and not just because he'd worked damn hard for his professional reputation or because of an overblown ego. He could deal with the kick in the ass. He couldn't handle disappointing his adoptive father, a man whom Doug owed his life. Doug was ten years old when his mother died and he'd been running from Social Services when Ted Houston had caught him trying to steal his wallet. Doug had figured he needed food in his stomach more than the guy with all the questions needed the cash in his pocket. Within the hour, he'd had Doug's life story and he'd taken Doug into his home and his heart.

That same heart was bad now and the stress of Doug's professional problems had taken a toll on the older man, and also on Doug's mother—the woman who'd raised him like her own son. Which meant Doug had to uncover whatever the Runaway Bride knew about her ex-fiancé and his shady dealings. If he scooped the other papers he'd be back on top. Doug wasn't ignorant and he knew clearing his name wouldn't fix his father's heart. But good news would give the older man an emotional boost, something the doctors said would help his mental state and drive for recovery. They were right. Just knowing Doug was out attempting to prove his claim had done wonders for his father's attitude. Enough to give Doug the push he needed to remain on the island and give this pretense a shot. And besides, he owed it to the *Tribune* and his boss to get accurate proof and cement his story.

So now, he awaited his prey. He knew what Juliette looked like thanks to the black-and-white photos in all the papers and the colored ones he'd seen in his research. He wouldn't be able to mistake the sleek, auburn hair, the chiseled profile or the elegant mannerisms ingrained in her by her public family. Until she'd bolted from the altar, Juliette had been perfection personified. And for Doug, a man intending to embark upon romance and discovery, she was both easy on the eyes as well as the libido.

Without warning, Merrilee, her assistant and a woman Doug had never seen before—but one he'd have no problem viewing again and again—walked into the lobby. Long spiral curls hung down her back in windblown disarray. Disheveled from the breeze and humidity, her hair had a tousled look, like that of a woman who'd just woken up after a night of hot sex. The moment when a woman was most soft, pliant and easily aroused. As aroused as he was now, just looking at her. Doug shifted his stance.

The white ruffle on her short denim miniskirt swayed provocatively in the humid breeze and the matching white, soft-looking cotton top dipped below one shoulder, revealing creamy white skin in stark contrast with fire-rich hair that screamed "touch me." And he wanted to.

Then she walked closer and he caught the chiseled profile surrounded by the auburn hair. High cheekbones. Pouty lips. Fire-rich hair—*auburn* hair.

His Runaway Bride.

He'd been so certain he'd know her on sight. He hadn't. And though he now realized she resembled her twin, Juliette was too distinctive to be identical to any other woman. It wasn't just the glorious mane of hair that had changed but the sense of liberation he saw both in her face and her more expressive mannerisms. Her hands flew in the air as she spoke to Merrilee. Her eyes glittered with surprise and awe as she took in whatever the older woman was saying.

She no longer resembled the conservative fiancée of Stuart Barnes or the biddable daughter of Senator Stanton. This woman had spark and intensity. Excitement burned inside of her.

She'd undergone a transformation since her almost-wedding and the reasons why intrigued him as much as the story itself.

Which said a lot for a man in search of the proof that would clear his name.

He wondered what it said about the outcome of his fantasy.

SECRET FANTASY. As her sister's students would say, "Well, duh." Juliette should have known by the name of the resort this wasn't just any island retreat. Better yet, she should have known when Gillian had elicited the promise that Juliette *let loose* that her twin was up to no good. And setting Juliette up for a week of decadence and sin—which was what being paired up with a sexy stranger would amount to—was definitely no good.

Or was it? Juliette gnawed on her lower lip, recognizing an opportunity to make up for all she'd missed by taking the safe and expected route all her life.

"Obviously you didn't sign on for this. If you decide to leave, I'll give you a full refund." Merrilee Schaefer-Weston shook her head and laughed. "Or should I say I'll give your sister a full refund? I must say this is a first for Fantasies, Inc." She reached out and touched Juliette's arm. "But, please, at least stay overnight as my guest. Perhaps the magic of the island will sway you."

Juliette glanced at the older but still beautiful owner of the complex. "Magic?" she asked wryly.

Merrilee's eyes danced with delight. "What else would you call a week away from prying eyes? A week solely for yourself, where no one will know what you say or do?"

"Except my fantasy man." Juliette shivered at the prospect of herself and an unknown stranger together for an entire erotic vacation. No Stuart, no scandal...

No reporters.

"I'll stay the week." Just like that she made her decision.

If Merrilee was surprised, she didn't show it. "Wonderful! You won't regret it."

Juliette hoped not. Because such spontaneity wasn't in her nature. But where had her preplanned, good-girl behavior gotten her? Used and jilted, in a manner of speaking. No one would believe normally conservative Juliette Stanton, a woman who thought out any and every move beforehand, would act on impulse. But as Merrilee said and her sister had ensured, Juliette now had that chance.

"Give me a moment and I'll see that you get checked in." Merrilee left her standing in the center of the lobby, an eclectic combination of lush tropical plants and ornate marble floor and pillars. A true island retreat.

She inclined her head and glanced to her left. A tingle of awareness took hold as she realized she was being watched—studied intently by an intriguing man with dark glasses and even darker hair. A well-toned man in swim trunks and nothing more. She swallowed hard.

He lifted his glasses and met her gaze. Her body grew hot from the inside out in a feminine way that had nothing to do with the humidity surrounding her.

"You're all set." Merrilee's voice surprised her. "We've got a secluded section of cottages that I'm sure you'll find to your liking."

Juliette regretfully withdrew her gaze from the stranger's compelling one. "I'm certain I'll love it and

appreciate you keeping me away from prying eyes."
She glanced back again, but he was gone. Disappointment, keen and lingering, settled inside her.

"Not to worry. I have a hunch you'll see him again," Merrilee said lightly.

"See who?"

Juliette knew she was playing dumb and Merrilee laughed. "Let me show you to the cottage. Your bags will follow shortly."

She accompanied the other woman out the open French doors and down a winding path, lined with green foliage and pink flowers Juliette couldn't name but loved on sight. As she passed the pool and various restaurants, her gaze searched restlessly for *him*.

Well, she thought, her sister believed she needed to get a life. Apparently she was about to find one.

2

AFTER A SHORT NAP and quick unpacking, Juliette changed and headed for the beach, stopping on the way to take in the view. Straight ahead, she glimpsed white sand and endless miles of blue water that stretched to the horizon, meeting an azure sky accented by puffy, white clouds. To her left, she found lush floral gardens and, to her right, a huge free-form pool with a cascading waterfall in its center.

"A veritable Garden of Eden," she murmured.

"Makes you think man was a fool for ever leaving."

The deep, masculine voice rumbled in her ear and she knew instinctively who stood beside her. Her heartbeat tripled and excitement churned her insides. "If I remember correctly, man didn't go by choice. He was banished."

"For tasting the forbidden fruit." At his words, a shiver of awareness took hold. She *had* to look.

And if he'd been sexy from afar, up close he was devastating. Without sunglasses, his eyes were a dynamic shade of blue, his features ruggedly handsome. Unlike her ex-fiancé's fair, all-American looks, this man was a rogue—from his dark hair, tanned skin and razor stubble, down to his baggy yet still sexy swim trunks.

Her fantasy come to life. In her dreams, this was the kind of man who came to her in the dead of night. The one who'd sweep her off her feet and make her the center of his world. No other agenda in sight.

He extended his hand. "Doug. And you are?"

"Pleased to meet you," she said with a hesitant smile. Being bold didn't come easily. "I'm Juliette." No last name attached, just as he hadn't offered his.

She placed her hand in his warm palm. The flare of heat was instant and intense. From the flicker of awareness in his eyes, he felt it too.

Startled by the strength of the attraction, she tried to withdraw but he held on tight. "Nice to meet you, Juliette."

His thumb brushed the pulse point on her wrist briefly before he let go. A rush of pleasure took hold, wrapping around her heart and warming her in ways she hadn't experienced in too long, if ever.

But she liked what she was feeling. Each tingling sensation in her body, every shimmer of awareness in her brain, she enjoyed. After the pain and heartache of the last few weeks, she realized she desperately needed to feel sexy and desirable. She craved the lavish attention that would assure her she wasn't second best. This man could provide that proof and be her much-needed diversion.

But one real and nagging fear remained. Although she'd escaped to this island, Juliette couldn't be certain she'd left the press behind. The last thing she wanted was to bring more scandal down on her father now.

Senator's Daughter's Secret Fantasy would be even worse than the Runaway Bride headlines. Thanks to his stellar reputation, the senator had weathered that gossip well and denied he'd been publicly embarrassed or cared about anything more than his daughter's well-being. But Juliette had no desire to shine more negative publicity on him during the last months of his tenure. The revelation about Stuart would be awful enough and she'd yet to figure out how to handle that.

But she was here, Juliette thought, and she deserved some private time. Looking into Doug's eyes, she felt his sincerity. The attraction was real, his attention singular and genuine. Unless she wanted to lose this once-in-a-lifetime opportunity, she had no choice but to put her fears aside and trust.

Unlike Stuart, Doug gazed at her as if she were special and, with everything inside her, Juliette wanted to grab onto what her sister had so generously given her. Juliette didn't wonder how Gillian had known what she needed. As twins they shared a bond stronger than anything tangible or understood.

"Where are you off to?" Doug asked, startling her out of her private thoughts.

"I was thinking of hitting the beach." She gestured towards the umbrellas dotting the sand below.

"And I was thinking of hitting on you." His lips

turned upward in a hesitant grin. "That is if you don't mind the company."

She met and held his gaze. When she'd decided to remain on Secret Fantasy, she'd decided to trust. She also had to let go of any inhibitions she normally felt. Upon unpacking, she'd discovered her sister had ransacked her suitcase and replaced the sensible items with impractical things and the conservative ones with sexy substitutes. Juliette was outwardly freed from constraint.

Her attitude had to follow. Easier said than done, and definitely easier to accomplish if she didn't look down at the cleavage her skimpy bathing suit exposed.

She cleared her throat. "As a matter of fact, I'd love company." She faltered, then reminded herself this man didn't know her. She could be anyone she wanted to be, act in new and exciting ways.

She held out her hand. He slid his warmer, larger palm against hers, curling his fingers around her skin. His touch was hot and electric, and like two pieces of a puzzle, they fit together.

Juliette didn't know if this was the man Merrilee had chosen for her fantasy, but after her lukewarm relationship with Stuart, she did know better than to ignore an attraction this strong and consuming. More than just sizzling chemistry differentiated him from her ex-fiancé. Where Stuart presented a civilized front, too civilized, she realized now, this man ex-

uded a raw power and wilder persona. All of which
tempted Juliette on a deeper, more sensual level.

She'd never felt like this before and probably never
would again. Why wait for another man to approach
her, one who couldn't compete with Doug? Juliette
didn't want some man that Merrilee had chosen for
her. She wanted this man and she intended to put in a
specific request of her own. She shivered beneath his
potent gaze. Whatever this week had in store, no
doubt she was in for a treat.

Doug held Juliette's hand as they walked toward
the beach. Questions assailed him from all sides. Who
was this woman who'd blindsided him on first sight?
Research, photographs and even distant glimpses
when she'd accompanied her fiancé to political func-
tions hadn't prepared him for reality. For the vibrant,
seductive woman with just the right hint of naïveté to
charm even a jaded reporter.

But he wasn't yet free to begin his quest. He was
still on probation in Merrilee's eyes and knew she
was concerned about his interest in her client. She'd
given him twenty-four hours so she could observe
and decide. He respected her reluctance and admired
her business sense. If the situation were reversed, he
might not be trusting himself right now.

In the meantime he had precious few hours to convince both women *he* was the only man for the job.
Persuading them wouldn't be a problem. Doug had
had plenty of experience charming women to get
what he needed.

"Where are you from?" Juliette asked.

The warmth and depth in her tone took him by surprise. He'd expected her voice to be more cultured and aloof, less gentle and kind. He suspected her personality would be soft to match. None of which boded well for Doug. Keeping an emotional distance would have been easier if she'd been like the icy politician's wives and the women in his past he'd grown used to dealing with.

"I'm from Michigan," he told her. Which he was, technically. Detroit born and raised until he was three months old. Then his father had split and his mother had moved them to Chicago.

But he couldn't place himself in Chicago because she might become wary and back off. Nor could he give her details like a last name in case she recognized him from his articles in the *Tribune*. So he'd skirt the outer boundaries of truth as best he could. The more honest he was, less chance of slipping up. The less of that damned guilt he hoped to feel.

She nodded. "I'm a Chicago native myself."

They strode down a set of wooden stairs and found themselves on soft white sand, facing the ocean. "This is unreal." She gestured toward the expanse of blue in front of them.

He turned toward her, took in her revealing swimsuit, a navy two-piece number that exposed generous cleavage, a flat stomach and incredibly long legs. He would have swallowed but his mouth had grown dry. "Yes, it is."

A warm blush burned her cheeks and Doug realized he'd made a mistake. Too forward, too soon.

He needed information, not sex. Well, hell. He shook his head. He was a man, wasn't he? If he was honest with himself he needed sex, too. But no matter how tempting he found her, how appealing, sex wasn't on his agenda. He was here to make her fantasy come true—to romance her and make her feel cherished while getting close enough for her to trust and confide in him about her ex-fiancé. Though her effect on him was powerful and strong, sex would be taking things between them too far, using her unfairly for selfish gains. He couldn't go that route again.

The notion surprised him. The Doug Houston he knew would go as far as he had to in order to get a story. Why should Juliette make things any different?

Because *she* was different. He didn't know why, but Juliette and her charming naïveté gave him a glimpse into himself and his less than stellar past. A past he'd be smart to learn from. Not only had he caused Erin immense pain by leading her on, but her vengeance was something he'd never forget. It was the reason he was on this damn island to begin with. But looking back, Doug couldn't wholly blame Erin. She'd had no reason to suspect he didn't want forever, if only because he'd never revealed himself. He'd slept with her because he'd been interested, stayed, he realized now, because she'd become convenient, both personally and professionally. But he hadn't loved her.

He glanced at his companion. Juliette Stanton was too beautiful, too *much*. Doug had a hunch if he got involved that way, *he'd* be the one on the receiving end of the kick in the stomach this time. Something he had no intention of experiencing.

He helped Juliette set up a chair and laid a towel across the slatted plastic straps. "Can I get you a drink?"

She shook her head. "I think I'll just take in the beauty surrounding me."

His gaze dipped from her flushed cheeks to the cleavage pushed upward by the sexy bathing suit. White mounds of flesh rose enticingly above the navy material. "I'd love to do the same." But he tamped down the urge to settle in beside her.

He'd made an impression. Enough for her first day. Hell, enough for his.

"Merrilee mentioned there's a beach party tonight."

At the sound of Juliette's excited voice, he turned. "Please don't tell me you're entering the wet T-shirt contest." His heart couldn't stand the strain.

"I think that would have the men begging Merrilee for a refund." A grin lifted the corners of her mouth but more than a hint of seriousness filled her gaze.

He shook his head and refrained from glancing downward, to where her full breasts nearly spilled over the triangular covering of her bathing suit. "I think you're underestimating your impact on the opposite sex."

"Oh, I think I'm pretty well aware of my impact on men." Her eyelashes fluttered closed, blocking her feelings and locking them away where he couldn't reach or see.

Doug eased himself onto the edge of the chair and sat beside her. "I'm not sure you do." He'd figured her run from the altar was painful, but her complete shutdown now gave him the distinct impression she'd seen or heard something from Stuart Barnes that left her doubting her allure.

Something that would bring her to this island in quest of a fantasy. He remembered everything in her file, but one thing most of all. She wanted to feel desirable. And he wanted to make her feel that way. He wanted to erase the doubt and shadows from her eyes and, for the first time in his jaded life, his motives weren't purely selfish.

He splayed one hand over her thigh, covering her flesh with his palm. "Why do I think you're being influenced by someone else's views?"

"Because you've been in the sun too long?" Wide, green eyes met his, genuine laughter in her voice.

Her playful side was back but he wasn't through with his mission. "I haven't been in the sun long enough to be delirious. On the other hand, I've been around you long enough to know how you affect me." His thumb brushed against her soft skin.

She sucked in a deep breath. "It's hot out here."

"Yeah, it is." And if he didn't move his hand, they'd both be getting hotter.

"I, uh, think you made your point." Her tongue darted out to coat her lips with moisture and he stifled a groan.

"I'm glad. Because I don't know you well but I can assure you, you'd affect any normal, living breathing guy."

She grinned. "That's good to hear. And as for not knowing me, we can remedy that." She shook her head, obviously embarrassed, causing long reddish-brown curls to cascade over one shoulder and settle above her breast.

"Are you inviting me?" he asked.

She blushed as she nodded. "I believe I am. To the beach party and to get to know me better." She averted her gaze. "Unless I'm being presumptuous."

That telling comment cemented his earlier hunch. Her provocative overtures didn't come easily. He realized how badly her pride and confidence had been battered. Although she'd walked out on the groom, she'd just reinforced his gut feeling that her hand had been forced and she'd taken an emotional beating in the process.

Moving his hand from the warmth of her thigh, he lifted her hand and enclosed it in his. "Well, Juliette, I most certainly *do* want your company tonight and I gratefully accept your invitation." He treated her to a slow, provocative grin meant to tease and tantalize. To draw her into the same vortex of interest and anticipation swirling inside him. To make her feel desired.

"Thank you." Her pink tongue darted across her lower lip once more, an intriguing combination of sensuality and innocence. Her forced daring was admirable, her hesitancy charming.

"Should I pick you up or meet you there?"

She curled her knees upward. "I have some things to take care of first. I'll meet you there, okay?"

He nodded. Walking away was more difficult than it should have been since he'd be seeing her again in a few hours. He'd never expected conservative Juliette Stanton to make the first move, especially after her initial withdrawal, but he couldn't deny she'd put him a step closer to his goal.

She'd given him entry into her week here on Secret Fantasy. She'd given him the chance to get his story. To find out what Juliette knew about her ex-fiancé's dirty business dealings. To discover whether Barnes was involved with the Mob and Haywood's money laundering scheme. To uncover the information to prove his earlier story was fact, not fiction.

Juliette had provided the opportunity. The rest was up to him.

MERRILEE SAT at her desk, staring at the large bouquet of red roses surrounded by baby's breath and greenery, specially delivered to her at Secret Fantasy. Apropos considering the card hadn't been signed, its sender anonymous, secret.

A knock sounded lightly on the closed wooden door to her office. "Come in."

The door swung open and Juliette Stanton walked inside, dressed as if she'd just come from the beach. "Hello. I'm sorry to disturb you but I was wondering if you had a minute— Oh, what lovely flowers!" She walked forward until she stood in front of the large floral bouquet.

"Thank you." Merrilee smiled. "I thought so too, though I do wish I knew who sent them," she murmured.

Juliette bent forward and inhaled the fragrant scent. "A secret admirer? How romantic!"

Merrilee inclined her head. "More like mysterious."

"Was there a card?" Juliette asked, then immediately waved her hand in the air. "I'm sorry. It's none of my business."

"Actually I've always felt once a person divulged their fantasies to me, a bond is created. I don't mind answering. There was a note." Merrilee lifted the standard-looking white card that had come attached to the flowers and read the inscription. "Roses, red as rubies. Because they're your favorite."

Juliette lowered herself into the armchair across from the desk. "And are they your favorite?"

Merrilee nodded. Because red rubies reminded her of Charlie, she thought, glancing down at her ring. But Charlie was long gone, as she knew too well. Getting sentimental and wistful over an intriguing gesture wouldn't bring him back. And though she wondered who knew her secrets, now wasn't the time to figure it out.

She pulled a tissue from the box on her desk and blotted beneath her eyes. "So what can I do for you?" she asked Juliette.

The younger woman's eyes filled with concern. "Maybe this isn't the best time. I can come back later."

Merrilee waved away her misgiving. "It's fine. I'm fine." She'd learned to be, of necessity. "Go on, please."

Juliette twisted her hands in her lap. "Well, I'm not familiar with how this fantasy stuff works but I have a request that may be...unorthodox."

Merrilee smiled to put her guest at ease. "Trust me, there's little I haven't seen or heard as the person in charge of making fantasies come true."

"Okay then." Juliette drew a deep breath. "I want Doug—I'm sorry I don't know his last name—but I want him as my fantasy man."

Doug. Merrilee knew Juliette meant Doug Houston and realized he'd chosen anonymity as a cover. After Doug's departure a week earlier, Merrilee had done some research of her own and was quite familiar with the behind-the-scenes story of this particular fantasy. She'd discovered, before agreeing to let him stay upon his second arrival, that he had told her the truth. One point in his favor but he was still on probation.

Merrilee understood now that if Juliette knew she'd chosen the man who'd printed the article on her ex-fiancé's business partner, she'd bolt. Maybe. But maybe attraction and desire were stronger than fear.

"The man from the lobby earlier?" she asked, just to be certain.

Juliette nodded. "Yes. I know you said I'd be seeing more of him and I want to. I want to make sure *he's* the man you've chosen for me. Unless he's already taken?" Juliette's eyes were wide as she waited for an answer.

"Obviously there's a strong attraction between you two."

Juliette blushed and averted her gaze. "I'm not sure I've ever felt this way before." She laughed uncomfortably. "Kind of like it hits you between the eyes and you're not certain what to do next."

"Except not let him get away?" Merrilee asked, both amused and pleased Juliette was responding so strongly to Doug.

She grinned. "Exactly."

The young woman had made Merrilee's decision that much simpler. Bound by confidentiality and ethics, she wasn't at liberty to reveal Doug Houston's background or relation to Juliette's recent past. That was for the two of them to work out, if and when the time came. But she'd studied Doug all afternoon and watched him around Juliette.

He might not be all he seemed, but Merrilee didn't believe he was looking to hurt Juliette. "Well, I don't see any problem. Whatever Doug's fantasy, and you understand I can't reveal that, it doesn't involve another woman."

Relief washed over Juliette. She hadn't realized how nervous she'd been that she'd lose Doug before she ever had him. "So he's..."

"Available."

She laughed. "I was going to say mine."

Merrilee leaned back in her seat. "Something tells me the man won't know what hit him."

Juliette grinned. "They say turnaround is fair play. As long as I'm giving in to the idea of this fantasy, I figured, why not try for the man who interests me most?"

"And I take it he's fulfilling *your* fantasy needs?"

"Making me feel like no one or nothing else is more important than me?" She nodded. "He's extremely good at that." And so much more. His intensity was incredible. A woman could go her whole life without being the sole focus of a man's attention. "I guess I owe my sister a thank-you for giving me this one week to enjoy and escape the problems back home."

Merrilee nodded. "My hope is that my guests leave here with a whole new perspective on life."

Juliette met Merrilee's understanding gaze. "I'm hoping to leave here with a whole new perspective on a lot of things."

"Well, if there's anything I can do, please stop by again."

She nodded. "Thank you. For everything. And until you find out who your secret admirer is, I hope you enjoy the attention."

Just as Juliette would enjoy Doug's.

Merrilee smiled, then stood, bracing her arms on the desk. "So, enjoy your stay at the resort, and let your fantasy begin."

"I certainly will." Juliette nodded, letting herself out of the office.

Her hand still on the cool doorknob, she recalled her time with Doug. For a split second this afternoon, she'd taken one look at such a good-looking man and nearly laughed at herself for thinking he'd be interested in her. Then she'd felt his hot hand against her thigh and his strong words of reassurance. She'd realized it was Stuart speaking inside her, making her doubt herself, stifling the confident woman she ought to be.

She'd allowed Doug to bring her confidence back because he cared enough to try. And caring was something she'd obviously missed out on—along with sexual tension and amazing chemistry. She thought about the upcoming week. Doug was a man who'd distract her from the dilemma over how and when to reveal her ex-fiancé's deceit. A man with whom she could cast away the safety net she'd hidden behind all her life and discover the sensual side of herself she'd believed was missing or nonexistent. A man she'd never see again after their time together.

And most important, a man who wasn't using her for her social or political connections.

JULIETTE STEPPED out of her cottage and into the humid night air. The floral scent she'd come to associate with the island hung heavy but, after the stifling isolation of home, she welcomed the fresh air and fragrant smells. She followed the narrow path that led from the isolated set of cottages to the beach where tonight's festivities awaited her. Where Doug awaited her, she hoped.

Torches lined the sandy shore and the orange glow of flames stood out in stark contrast to the inky night sky. She stepped down the rickety wooden stairs and paused. A bonfire burned on one section of the beach and a band playing Beach Boys type music rocked on a makeshift stage. People mingled, some in pairs, others in groups, a few individuals wandered alone. She wasn't in the mood to socialize with complete strangers, except maybe one in particular. She narrowed her gaze and searched through the crowd.

"Looking for someone?" *His* voice sounded from behind her.

Her heartbeat immediately doubled. "Just taking in the sights."

"If you say so." He laughed.

The deep, masculine sound caused ripples of warmth to ooze through her veins.

"But I know I was looking for you." His voice held a gentle heat, but it was his word choice that warmed her.

"You found me. I was just about to take a look around."

"Sounds good to me." He gestured with a sweep of his hand, indicating she should go first.

Two strides and she reached the sand where waiters, dressed in baggy shorts and colored T-shirts, stood ready to serve. Juliette continued forward, but Doug grabbed her hand, pulling her aside. "One thing before we check things out."

She inclined her head. "What's that?"

He braced his hands on her shoulders, pulling her gently toward him. Razor stubble covered his cheeks, thick and alluring, while his eyes, as blue as the ocean, stared into hers. "Thank you for inviting me to spend the night with you."

"Now who's being presumptuous?" she asked.

His eyes opened wide, as he apparently realized what he'd just said and Juliette laughed.

Laugh lines wrinkled around his eyes. "Something tells me not to touch that statement."

"Not yet, but there's time." She laughed nervously, wanting to give him a green light but uncertain of how to proceed. Yet his intensity and obvious interest made her brave when she might have withdrawn.

"I'm not going anywhere."

And neither was she. The irony wasn't lost on her though. She was a woman who'd learned from early childhood *not* to reveal too much about herself and to maintain proper decorum at all times lest the press print vile, ugly stories. Yet here she was at the most difficult crossroads of her life opening up enough to

trade sexual innuendo with a gorgeous stranger—
and not caring a bit.

Juliette drew a calming breath but she inhaled his
masculine scent and realized little could still the emotions rampaging inside her, the increased beat of her
heart and the building crescendo of excitement.

"Cocktail?" A waiter paused, a variety of multicol-
ored drinks on his tray.

"Piña Colada? Tequila Sunrise?" Doug narrowed
his gaze and assessed the assortment. "Or would you
like me to go over to the bar and get something else?"

"You choose."

He took two tall glasses off the tray, handing her a
cream-colored drink, and taking one for himself. The
waiter moved on, leaving them alone. "Piña Colada."

She accepted the cool glass and tasted the frothy
drink. "Mmm. It's sweet," she said, surprised, then
licked at her flavored lips with her tongue.

He laughed. "I figured I'd start you off slow."

"What gave me away?"

"Your huge, curious eyes for one thing. You eyed
that tray like you'd never seen anything like it before."

She ducked her head, embarrassed at her less than
worldly ways. "I'm more familiar with wines and
champagne." Fun drinks were a novelty she'd never
experienced.

"Something tells me you've lived a very sheltered
life."

She shrugged. "More like an ultraconservative one.

But my twin—she's experienced it all." Juliette changed the subject to Gillian, finding it easier to talk about her sister than let her own lack of experience intrude on the fantasy.

"Well, after this week, you'll be able to claim the same."

A grin edged the corners of her mouth. "I'm happy to say we're on the same wavelength. I'm here to experience it all." Everything he had to offer. "So what else are you going to introduce me to?"

A tremor wracked Doug's body. No way did she really want to know what new and enlightening experiences he'd like to share with her. Experiences that would never, could never, pass the bounds of fantasy. No sex, he reminded himself.

But damn, he needed something to distract him from the come-hither looks she covertly sent his way. Despite her provocative comeback, the tremor in her voice and her huge eyes gave her true nature away. As a senator's daughter, she'd grown up in front of the camera and had learned how to maintain polish and poise. But here on the island, faced with real desire, she radiated a naïveté he hadn't expected. He didn't think she could possibly be aware of her hungry gaze or the effect it was having on him.

But he knew. And every time he took in the outfit she'd chosen, his mouth grew dry. The sarong-style skirt tied at one hip revealed an expanse of long, bare leg while the bikini-like top exposed her flat, untanned stomach and accentuated her full, rounded breasts. No different than the clothing worn by most women on the beach tonight, but most women weren't Juliette. And none of them affected him in the same beguiling way.

The woman was more of a feast than the one prepared by Merrilee's staff. "Let's check out the bamboo huts." He pointed to where makeshift food stations had been set up beneath the thatched roofs, smorgasbord style. "Nothing like choices. What do you want? Hamburgers, hot dogs or do you want to try the Floridian specialty, conch fish?"

Juliette inhaled the assorted smells, wrinkling her nose when the distinct odor of fish came through loud and clear. "I think I'll stick with your basic burger."

He laughed. "I guess conservative girls don't appreciate the art of catching, scaling and gutting a fish."

She sniffed as if offended, but the smile on her gloss-covered lips gave her away. "I didn't say I was conservative, I said I lived a conservative life. Big difference. As for you, you're so relaxed, I don't see an ounce of conventionality in you or your upbringing. Am I right?"

"Quite right." And perhaps if he revealed some of his own past, she'd be more comfortable revealing hers. "I was adopted and neither set of parents were what you'd call conservative."

"I'd say not, especially if you inherited either of their style of dress." She reached out and fingered the bottom of his long, Hawaiian-print shorts before raising her gaze to his clashing but equally tropical button-down, short-sleeve shirt.

"Offensive?" he asked.

"Different," she said with a grin. She twirled one of her long curls around her finger.

He wondered if the strands were silky smooth to the touch and when he'd be able to find out. "Different how?"

"Where I come from, men wear power suits and ties or polo shirts and slacks."

Bingo, he thought. Some insight. Small as it may be, he appreciated any inroad. "Well, if anyone in my family does the suit-and-tie thing I've never seen it."

Ted Houston never wore a suit, not even when he'd won an Associated Press award. Good thing his father's byline hadn't been in politics. Doug, on the other hand, knew how to dress up with the best of them, but on the island he'd chosen to let his rebel side dominate. To throw Juliette off his proverbial scent. Disgusted with the reminder and unsure why, when his pursuit of a story had never bothered him before, Doug pushed the thought away—easy to do when surrounded by her beauty.

He smiled, then lifted his shoulders in a shrug. "My adoptive father is color-blind. I guess I inherited the gift."

She laughed at his joke.

He shut his eyes for a moment, allowing himself to enjoy the light, carefree sound. Just being around her helped him relax for the first time, not just since the paper fiasco, but since his father's heart attack. He hadn't realized how much he needed the release until she'd provided it.

"Hey, don't get me wrong, your style is a welcome change."

At the sound of her soft voice, he opened his eyes.

"You're a welcome change," she said.

And damned if he didn't believe her.

She paused for another sip of her drink. The waiter had forgotten the straws or Doug hadn't seen them on the tray. Either way, he didn't care. It gave him a chance to touch her. He reached out and brushed the foam off her upper lip with the pad of his thumb.

She stilled, those wide, green eyes meeting his, shock evident in her gaze. He recognized the emotion since he felt it, too. His mind told him to use the surprising electric connection that sizzled between them to his advantage since, except for her one vague reference, she'd adeptly avoided any personal replies to his light queries. She had even managed to turn the tables and question him instead. But his heart pounded loud in his chest, urging him merely to enjoy.

He drew back and as she watched, he licked the sweet-tasting froth off his finger. She exhaled, a slow, breathy sound that resembled a sigh of pleasure and his body tensed in response.

Just then, dinner was announced over the sound system, directing people to the buffet and jarring him back to his senses. He'd missed a perfect opportunity to push for information under the guise of getting to know her better. Not only didn't he understand why, but he was completely off balance. "Saved by the bell," he muttered.

"Excuse me?"

He shook his head. "Nothing. How about we get something to eat?"

She nodded. "Sounds like a plan."

A good one because he needed distance. And how much trouble could he get into over the course of one meal?

Half an hour later he had his answer. Too much damn trouble. With food loaded on their plates, they walked by the long picnic tables set up for guests and, at Juliette's suggestion, headed farther down the beach. She picked a secluded area and requested he pull two lounge chairs together for their private picnic.

Doug was coming to realize he couldn't deny her anything when she got that excited gleam in her eye. In one short outing, he'd learned to recognize the sparkle that told him she was experiencing something for the first time—from a simple drink to a picnic dinner. He'd grown up quickly, first on the street experiencing deprivation, then at Ted Houston's side, learning the journalistic ropes from a pro. He'd discovered how to charm the devil himself for information or to gain access to private files or events. From the streets to formal banquets and affairs, Doug had seen it all.

But he'd never lived Juliette's existence, never realized living a sheltered life could cause a person to miss out on so much. To his surprise, he was grateful he was giving her good memories to replace the more recent painful ones. Ones he'd inadvertently caused. He just wished watching her wasn't so difficult.

Arousingly difficult. She licked her fingers delicately before turning to the napkin in her lap and wiping her hands. She set the napkin aside and yawned, then said, "It's not the company, I swear."

"It's the travel. I'm surprised you've made it this late. Did you want to watch the pathetic rendition of the Beach Boys or call it a night?" He didn't know which he hoped she'd choose but a night to rethink his strategy wouldn't be a bad thing.

She sighed. "Much as I hate to say this, I think turning in would be best."

Disappointment warred with relief. "I understand."

After they collected and deposited their paper goods and garbage, she turned toward him. "I really enjoyed tonight."

"Me too. But until I walk you to your door, it's not over." He wasn't ready to let her go yet and hoping for a glimmer of information wasn't the only reason.

"You don't need to do that. But I'd like it if you would."

And he'd like to take a jump into the cool ocean

water. Walking her to her secluded cottage door, he felt more like a kid on his first date than an experienced reporter out to get a story. But Rome wasn't built in a day and neither would he get what he needed tonight.

"Well, we're here." She turned around, her back against the door, palms braced behind her.

From the gleam in her eye he wouldn't get a fast escape and a quick good-night. From his body's response to this woman, he didn't want one.

Her fantasy, he reminded himself. He'd worked damned hard to discover it—for his own selfish purposes, he admitted to himself. But now when the time came to make her feel both desired and cherished, his reasons for doing so were no longer cut and dried. He enjoyed giving her the attention and reveled in knowing he put that sexy gleam in her eyes.

Doug stepped forward and stroked her cheek with his hand. She sighed and, on impulse, he twirled one long curl around his finger. Her hair was as silky smooth as he'd thought but her skin was softer.

He tugged gently, bringing her closer, her lips within kissing distance. Would they feel as supple and delicate as her flesh? Or would the brief good-night kiss he intended blaze out of control, treating him to a firmer, more powerful touch of her mouth against his? He'd promised himself to keep his distance and still swore sex would never come into play—not if he was using her as a means to uncover information.

But kissing her now had nothing to do with his story and everything to do with his need—for her. He leaned in until his mouth covered hers. And then he knew. Her lips were soft but determined. They carried a sweetness from their last shared Piña Colada and a gentleness he'd expected. But she greeted his overture with a lack of hesitancy and an eagerness which shouldn't have taken him off guard. But it did.

She did. All his strength went into maintaining a seductive kiss that left her wanting more. Hell, he knew how badly *he* wanted more. As if she read his mind, her lips parted in invitation. His tongue slipped inside her warm, moist mouth, a sigh of pure pleasure reverberated in her throat and his body shook in reaction. He moved forward without thought, locking her between him and the cottage door. Her hands moved to cup his waist, her nails digging into him despite the barrier of clothing.

For a brief moment, he let her body mold to his. For a brief moment, he allowed her to feel what she did to him. And then, in what had to be the most difficult move of his life, he stepped back and broke the kiss first. But he wasn't ready to break the connection between them. He rested his forehead against hers and listened to her labored breathing, a perfect match for his rapidly beating heart.

"You're good," she murmured.

Doug couldn't help it—he laughed. "You're not so bad yourself." He raised his head and met her soft, hazy stare.

Reaching out, she swiped at his damp lips with one finger. A tremor of awareness lodged in his throat.

"I'll take that as a compliment," she said.

"I meant it as one." His lips tingled from her touch and his mind filled with conflicting thoughts. "You should get some sleep." And he should back off and regroup.

He withdrew the room key from her hand and pushed open the door. But he remained outside as she passed by him and whispered a soft good-night in his ear.

Doug actually trembled as she shut the door behind her. "Damn." He needed a new strategy and he needed one fast.

Otherwise he was in danger of losing himself in Juliette Stanton and ignoring the burning need for information. A need she too easily made him forget.

3

JULIETTE ROLLED OVER, surprised to realize it was morning already. One of the perks of this resort was the luxury of not sleeping in a typically uncomfortable hotel bed. The mattress was as firm as the one at home, the pillows ample and comfortable. She reached her arms out wide and stretched, waking her tired muscles. The bed was large enough for two and she'd lain awake last night wishing she weren't alone. Wishing she'd had the courage to invite Doug inside.

But she hadn't asked and he hadn't suggested, by innuendo or otherwise. He was a gentleman—she liked that about him. He was taking things slow—she had mixed feelings about that.

She forced herself to rise and head for the bathroom. Intellectually, she understood it was Stuart's betrayal that made her doubt herself and her desirability but she couldn't deny the resulting need to have Doug prove he was as interested in her as she was in him.

When it came to this man, her desires were far from satisfied and she wasn't just talking physically. She wanted to get to know him better, too. She wanted to know what his fantasy was and whether she was an integral part of its fulfillment. And since one-night stands weren't her style, she appreciated the chance to get to know him better before jumping into intimacy she wasn't emotionally ready for.

After splashing cold water on her face and brushing her teeth, she was awake if not ready to tackle the day. A knock sounded at her door and she jumped in surprise before remembering she'd hung the room service card on her door late last night.

"Coming!" On a full stomach and caffeine, she could better deal with the beach, the bikinis and Doug, not necessarily in that order.

She headed for the closet to search for something to put on over her short nightie. She already knew the long, terry robe she'd packed herself was gone, in its place a short, silk wrap courtesy of Gillian—an inappropriate garment to answer the door in. Juliette rifled through the clothes, hoping for sweats or something with more coverage, but her sister had made sure comfortable was replaced by sexy.

The knock came again, louder this time. "Coming," she called once more.

She sighed and grabbed for the short robe. It was this or her nightie and there was no contest there. She wrapped the cool, satin-feeling garment around her, knotting the belt as she walked.

She opened the door quickly before the waiter left along with her food. But the man standing before her wasn't a waiter.

It was Doug. Her heart leapt at the sight of him and

Juliette knew she was in deep. He wore the sunglasses he'd had on the first time she noticed him, but, up close, with razor stubble on his face and a sensual grin on his lips, he gave new meaning to the word sexy.

And knowing she'd kissed those same lips... She shivered and, without thinking, pulled the lapels of her robe together—as if anything could protect her from his potent effect.

As if she even wanted protection, she thought wryly. He tipped his head forward, and despite the dark glasses, she knew he'd noted her attempt to cover herself, felt his heated gaze travel over her skin and brand her.

"You ordered room service?" he asked.

She'd been so entranced by seeing him, only now did she realize he not only carried a breakfast tray, but also a bouquet of exotic flowers beneath his arm. She'd worried whoever was at her door would lose patience and walk away, but by Doug's intense expression he wasn't going anywhere anytime soon.

He extended the flowers and she accepted them, inhaling the fragrant scent. "Thank you."

"You're welcome." He cleared his throat. "I can put the tray on the terrace and we can eat there, we can eat inside, or I can put it on the dresser and leave you in peace, but have pity on me because the darn thing's getting heavy." His lips turned upward in a slow grin that was part reluctant but completely sexy.

He had this fantasy thing down pat. She doubted

he knew exactly what her fantasy was, but she couldn't deny he was fulfilling her every whim. He knew just how to cater to her and make her feel special, knew exactly how to set her up as the center of his universe. And if Juliette had to guess, he wasn't at all worried about her asking him to leave. After last night, why should he be? She wanted him here as much as he apparently wanted to stay.

She treated him to a smile of her own. "If I'm going to have breakfast beneath the warm sun overlooking an exotic garden of tropical plants, I'd hate to do it alone. The terrace door is open. Why don't you set the tray there?" She let her hand fall to her side and her robe parted as if on command, exposing the lacy-edged nightgown and nothing more.

Although his eyes darkened with interest, Juliette knew she hadn't revealed much.

Except her desire to have him around.

Doug let out a long breath. He'd thought a good night's sleep would give him perspective, distance and a renewed vigilance to dig for information and dig deep. He was a professional and his father needed him home. He had plenty of reason to give his full attention to his goal. He'd even brushed aside the possibility that Merrilee might not allow him to stay on. He needed to be here too badly to think about that now.

But as he took in Juliette's soft, sexy robe he knew remaining detached wasn't something he could accomplish easily. His plan for the day would keep them busy and give him the opportunity for get-to-know-you conversation and hopefully some revelations in between. But he still had to deal with *now*. And one glance at how she looked first thing in the morning shifted his focus. He no longer wanted to talk because a different desire had taken hold.

He'd already acknowledged his weakness for soft, sexy women. And Juliette, fresh from her bed and achingly beautiful, tempted him to put his baser needs ahead of his more pressing ones. Before he could act on an impulse he'd regret, he headed inside and, ignoring the open bedroom door and the rumpled bed in which she'd slept, he went straight for the terrace and the welcoming breeze.

"I've fantasized about this." Her husky voice sounded behind him.

"About rolls and butter?" He lifted the tray and revealed her breakfast selection. Better than delving into the subject of real fantasies with a half-dressed woman he desired.

"About eating breakfast on a tropical island with a gorgeous man by my side." She held on to the slider door with one hand and swung around until she'd joined him on the courtyard overlooking the gardens. "And how can you call a continental breakfast just rolls and butter?"

She settled into a white wrought-iron chair, crossing her legs and revealing an expanse of skin that had him drooling for far more than the food on the tray.

"Because I prefer sweets," he said. He couldn't control his tone of voice, deepened by her effect on him.

She picked up a strawberry from the side dish of fresh fruit. "Sweet like this?" she asked, twirling the ripe, red berry between two fingers. "Or more like this?" She lifted a sugar-coated pastry from the basket.

"No." He walked to where she sat. Bracing his hands on the arms of her chair, he leaned over her, close to her mussed hair and fresh skin. "More like this." He brushed his lips over hers, meaning to keep things light.

And he did. Featherlight and teasingly soft, he managed to maintain control—until she sighed. A soft sigh that did him in. His knees nearly buckled. Hell, if not for his grip on the chair, he'd have fallen at her feet, and *that* was a first. But he held on to his dignity and allowed himself a long, lingering taste of her luscious mouth before forcing himself back.

He lifted his head and found her studying him, a smile on her well-kissed lips. "Sweet enough?" she asked.

"For now." He shrugged, his attempt at nonchalance pathetic, he knew. But now that he'd had an appetizer, maybe he could call himself satisfied and get down to business. He ignored the voice in his head branding him a fool and moved around to the opposite side of the table, settling himself across from her. "So, are you enjoying your vacation?"

"More each passing minute." Her lips twitched with the effort to withhold a smile. She had him and she obviously knew it. "Coffee?"

He nodded. "But let me. I'm catering this meal for you, remember?" He reached for the carafe.

"You brought the food, but that doesn't mean I can't help serve. I'm not some helpless female."

He leaned back, folding his arms behind his head. "In that case, I'd love a cup of coffee. Black."

She grinned and took the white carafe off the tray and filled his cup.

"So you're not a helpless female and I already know you're not a feminist—"

"How would you know that?" She poured herself coffee and added a small amount of milk, stirring while she awaited his answer.

"Because I took your key, held the door open for you last night and lived to tell about it."

She laughed. "Think what you want but if you ever step on my rights, you *will* hear about it."

He tucked her warning away for later thought. It wasn't something he could let himself think about and still do his job. "I have no doubt you can stand up for yourself. But back to my original question. You're not helpless and you're not a radical feminist," he said, amending his earlier statement. "Then what are you?"

"In real life?" She ripped off a piece of donut and popped the sugar-laden treat into her mouth. She pointed to her stuffed cheeks and held up one finger.

Stalling. He recognized the tactic. "Yes, in real life. I don't plan on letting the world intrude but I would like to get to know you a bit." He lowered his voice. "I'd like you to get to know me, too." And he meant it, Doug realized.

As much as he could share with her, he wanted to. He'd spent his youth relying on himself, and even after the Houstons had brought him home, he'd been afraid to let them in. It had taken much patience on each of his adoptive parents' part to gain access to his heart. Yet here was Juliette, a woman he'd just met, a woman who probably possessed information he needed, and Doug found himself wanting to open up as much as he wanted to listen to her in return. He shook his head in frustration, knowing his reasons transcended the charade he'd been forced to play out here on Secret Fantasy. She was getting to him and that put his story and his heart in danger.

The charade he'd willingly begun and needed to continue, his internal editor silently corrected. "I'll make it easy for you and tell you something about me first. I'm a writer." He leaned back in his chair and took a sip of his coffee.

She swallowed the last of her donut. "I'm a PR consultant for a pharmaceutical company," she said. "And I'm single."

He nearly choked on his coffee.

"I just thought you'd want to know." She batted her lashes in a deliberate attempt to flirt and have fun.

He grinned. "Same here. I'm single, I mean."

"Ever married before?"

"Nope." That she'd delve into personal subjects surprised him and opened the door for questions of his own.

"Ever come close?" She asked before he could toss the question back at her.

Damn, she was good. She knew how to hit a question dead-on and leave him squirming in his seat. The woman had journalistic instincts she knew nothing about. He eyed her closely. She'd settled in, obviously content to eat her breakfast and wait until he decided to answer.

He let out a groan because he wanted to confide in her, yet sharing his secrets was in direct opposition to his goals. Still, he answered her anyway, not glancing away and not hiding his feelings from her curious eyes. "Is it possible to come close if you never intended to marry in the first place?"

"It is if you got caught up in the swing of things." And Lord knew Juliette could understand *that*. She'd been so wrapped up in what she thought was reality, she'd been blinded to the truth.

"More like I got involved in a relationship where we each wanted different things only neither one knew it until it was too late." His heavy sigh settled around her.

"Too late for what?" She leaned forward, needing to hear his answer. Needing to know she wasn't the only one who could be fooled and betrayed.

His deep gaze locked onto hers. "Too late for someone not to get hurt." His stare never wavered, his voice was strong and full of remorse.

Juliette let out a breath of air. "I know what that's like."

He tipped his head to the side, curiosity and something more in his eyes. "Guess we have that in common at least."

"Mmm." She didn't know what had possessed her to question him on subjects she wanted to avoid herself but, like him, she was glad to see they shared an emotional connection. Glad to see they could relate on a personal level. But she wasn't ready to divulge more, no matter how close she wanted them to get.

He shifted in his seat. Gearing up for a question in return? Juliette didn't know but she had to back off. Now, before he turned the tables on her. She wiped her mouth with the napkin and placed it on the table. "So what do you have planned for today?"

His stare lingered and she sensed his reluctance to drop the discussion. But he pushed back his chair and stood, offering his hand for her to accept. "I thought we'd try some of the activities the resort offers."

"Safety in numbers?" she asked wryly.

He laughed but didn't look her in the eye. "Anyone ever tell you you're too perceptive for your own good?"

"Not recently." Nor would the events in her life back up his claim.

"Well, don't let other people's opinions make you sell yourself short."

Talk about perceptive, she thought. She'd been measuring herself by Stuart's standards for too long. "I need to shower and change."

"And I have some things to take care of with Merrilee."

Regarding his fantasy or just his stay on the island? Juliette narrowed her eyes, dying to ask. But she remained silent, knowing that if she respected the parameters of his fantasy, he'd do the same for hers. They never had to discuss her failings or the reason for her trip here—unless she wanted to confide in him. A shocking possibility.

"Let me walk you out."

He shook his head. "You relax. I'll head around the side of the cottage and meet up with you later."

She smiled. "I hope so."

He rose from his seat. "Count on it." He treated her to a wink that sent tremors of heated awareness straight to the pit of her stomach.

She watched him leave, his cut-off denim shorts molding to his firm backside and his ragged short-sleeve sweatshirt revealing tanned, muscular arms. Good Lord, the man was sexy.

His character and strength had her stomach twisting in conflicting knots. Safe or not, stupid or not, she wanted all he had to offer. She wanted to attain her deepest desire. And for the moment, her needs were simple.

She wanted to be held in his arms. She wanted him to make her feel, not just desired, but also secure, something she had a hunch he'd do with ease. And she wanted to admit the pain in her life and let him help her heal.

He was the perfect man for the job, considering he knew about sharing and confiding. He'd given her a glimpse inside his soul, something Stuart had never done. In all their time together he'd never once looked at her so intently or discussed anything emotional. Except his campaign, she thought wryly.

Doug was different. He couldn't possibly be faking the warmth in his eyes or caring in his expression. Although he was here to make her fantasy come true, she sensed she was learning about him as well. And her instincts screamed for her to trust him, stronger and more passionately than her gut instinct had ever believed in Stuart.

Having made a huge mistake last time, Juliette wasn't planning on rushing into anything now. She had time to learn about Doug and relearn to trust herself as well. She could, and would, test her feminine wiles and her ability to tease and arouse, both Doug as well as herself. And when she finally made love with him—and oh, how she wanted to—the experience would be the answer to her dreams.

In the meantime, anticipation was half the fun, something Doug obviously understood well. He was building their romance slowly, with deep, drugging kisses and intimate gestures like flowers and breakfast.

And she was hoping for much, much more.

DOUG NEEDED a breather. He made his way to the beach and kicked back in a lounge chair, letting the ocean waves and the cooler morning breeze soothe his nerves and his conscience. After leaving Juliette, he'd called home to check on his father.

The older man hadn't been released from the hospital; in fact, the doctor was running more tests. His mother insisted Doug stay on assignment because his father's mood had greatly improved since Doug's departure and promise to return with good news. And, besides, nothing more could be done until the tests came back and they decided whether to treat with medication or surgery. So, for now, his father was resting comfortably. But Doug wasn't.

Doug had seen Juliette's eyes light up when she found him on her doorstep, breakfast and flowers in hand. And his own heart had taken a huge leap upon seeing her again after only one short night apart. All real, not part of the fantasy.

"Good morning, Mr. Houston." Merrilee's voice sounded from behind him, then she walked around and pulled an upright chair beside his. "Enjoying the peace and quiet?" she asked.

"I'm enjoying everything about this place."

"Thank you." Pride infused her voice. "I'm sure you've been wondering what my decision is."

"I trust your judgment. I'm hoping you can bring yourself to trust me." He wanted to grin, to charm her with a smile, but he couldn't muster the false sentiment. Damned if he could understand what was overcoming him this trip.

She crossed one leg over the other and rested her weight on one side, facing Doug. "Interesting you should be so astute as to pick up on the fact that trust has to go both ways. I'm counting on you to remember that when you're with Juliette."

Doug thought about his discussion with Juliette earlier. "She's smart. Smart enough to get information out of me without me questioning her in return." Ever been married before? she'd asked. Ever come close?

Why hadn't he just asked her those same questions in a natural flow of conversation? He'd never let an opportunity slip by in the past, yet he had now—because he didn't want to watch a shutter fall down over her honest and expressive eyes again. There it was again, that innocence and naïveté that called to him in ways he didn't understand. If Doug wasn't careful, he could easily end up wanting her trust more than he wanted information, and that he couldn't afford. Damn.

Merrilee laughed. "Are you saying you've met your match?"

He refused to touch that comment. "Are you telling me I can stay?" He sat up in his seat and met her on level ground.

Her warm eyes danced with delight. "Mr. Houston, I wouldn't miss this for the world. But make no mistake, if you hurt Juliette Stanton instead of making her happy during her time on my island, you'll answer to me and my lawyers."

Doug ignored the unwelcome shaft of guilt over his hidden agenda. He might not understand it, but here on Secret Fantasy, he'd grown used to the sentiment.

He attempted to assuage his conscience by telling the truth instead. "You have my word. I'm not looking to hurt Juliette Stanton." He extended his hand, gripping Merrilee's in a strong shake.

She nodded. "Please come to my office and sign the paperwork documenting your fantasy," she said, her voice softening.

"My pleasure. I noticed some people disembarking from the seaplane. Are you fully booked this week?"

"I've been fortunate in that since opening the resorts, I'm booked solid every week, though I've fit some people in toward the end of this week who seem more desperate than most. I'll do that sometimes, if the person strikes a chord with me."

Doug grasped her hand. "Something tells me most people strike that chord. You're a rare breed—an honest, caring soul."

She laughed. "And you're a charmer. But actually, I'm an old soul. Lived and seen enough to understand other people's joy...and pain. Enough to make this place a success, I suppose."

"Forgive me for being blunt but I noticed a sadness in your eyes the first time we met."

She smiled, the lines around her eyes giving her face more mature beauty and character. "You're a reporter. I don't expect much to miss those eagle eyes. But you're right." She glanced down, toying with a fringe on her long skirt. "I lost my fiancé in the Vietnam War. I married afterward but it wasn't the same. I spent my life catering to someone else's needs at the expense of my own." She looked up, meeting his curious gaze.

"Seems to me that opening these resorts accomplishes the same thing."

"Ah, but I get pleasure watching other people's fantasies come to life and play out. Nine times out of ten the end result isn't what they intended, but often better than they'd hoped."

Doug laughed, enjoying this woman and her philosophy of life. "Sounds cryptic."

"Talk to me again when the week's out." She rose from her seat and Doug followed. "But don't hesitate to stop by my office when the whim strikes. I like you, Doug Houston."

"The feeling's mutual."

She patted his hand. "Then don't disappoint me."

She ambled off down the beach and he exhaled a groan. She didn't ask for more than she had a right to expect. Hell, she didn't ask for more than he demanded from himself. Yet he couldn't shake the feeling he was treading very shaky personal ground. And Merrilee knew it.

On his way out of the main lobby, he stopped at the concierge to make arrangements for a special evening. When he'd gotten access to Juliette's Fantasies,

Inc. paperwork, he'd discovered more about her than he'd ever dreamed. He knew not only the things she feared, like water skiing, but things she'd love to try, from hot-air ballooning to horseback riding on the beach. In an effort to broaden the possibilities of her guests' fantasies, Merrilee's questions were broad and thorough enough to give Doug a boost in his quest to make Juliette's experience one she'd never forget. Hell, Doug knew he wouldn't forget one minute of his time here.

After setting up the evening, he headed for the pool. The entire area was already filled with people and towels on the chairs, but Doug had an easy time spotting Juliette in the eclectic mix. No one else had her shade of hair and no other woman attracted him so strongly.

When he joined her at the far end of the free-form pool in a space with ample privacy, he realized she'd fallen asleep. He pulled over a chair from a neighboring table and sat facing her, propping his feet on the edge of her lounge. For the first time in his life Doug, a man always on the move, was content to sit in silence and watch a woman sleep.

Her chest rose and fell in even breaths, her breasts full, her nipples tight against the bikini top. In contrast to the sexy sight of her lush body in the skimpy bathing suit, her makeup-free face glistened with suntan oil and her mouth was opened slightly, giving her an innocent appearance that touched something inside his more world-weary soul.

He crossed his hands over his stomach and studied her, wondering why she appealed to him so. Just then her eyelashes fluttered and she let out a sigh, shifting restlessly. He reached out a hand to soothe her with a caress, then withdrew as she settled down before he touched her. He wondered if she was dreaming and if so about what. Or whom.

Minutes later she woke with a start. A shiver shook her, despite the heat, and he watched, entranced, as awareness of her surroundings dawned slowly. "You're awake."

Startled, she turned toward him, a light blush on her already sunburned cheeks. "How did, when did you get..." She shook her head. "Never mind. I'm sure I don't want to know."

He laughed, not at her discomfort but because he enjoyed her so much. "I've only been here a short while and, in case you're curious, you don't snore."

"Gee, thanks."

"Did you have a good rest?"

She nodded, then quickly averted her gaze, making him wonder again about those dreams she might have had. "Are you still interested in those resort activities?"

She curled her knees up beneath her chin. "You bet. After a swim and cool drink. What did you have in mind?"

"Beach volleyball and then a surprise."

She grinned. "I *love* surprises."

"Then let's get the day started. I'll race you to the

pool." He pulled his shirt over his head and tossed it on top of her beach bag on the ground.

Her wide-eyed gaze followed his movement, her stare settling on his bare chest.

"You keep looking at me like that and even the pool won't cool me off."

"There're more ways than a pool to take care of your problem." Her eyes darkened with a heat he couldn't mistake.

For the first time in their acquaintance she didn't look away when tossing out a provocative comeback. And though a light blush stained her cheeks, determination shone in her eyes and no tremor shook her voice. She was comfortable around him, he realized. Enough to let down her guard. The initial awkwardness was gone.

Heaven help him now.

4

JULIETTE DOVE into the heated pool, the water still cool enough to jolt her back into reality and out of the sensual haze her dream had taken her into. And what a dream she'd had. Centering around Doug and his erotic talents, all of her senses had been heightened and aroused. She'd fallen asleep thinking about him, so her dream made sense on a logical level. But in her imagination, he had taken her to a fevered, unsatisfied state of desire and she'd awakened, her yearning high, to find he'd been watching her as she slept.

As she rose from the depths of the deep end, pushing her hair back and shaking the water from her face, Doug surfaced beside her. "How about that drink?" He pointed toward the cascading waterfall and the tropical water bar.

"I think I'll wait awhile." No telling how her body would react to a combination of alcohol, sun and Doug. She leaned back and floated on top of the water, letting the rays bathe her face in warmth.

"How about sharing a raft instead?"

She lifted her head to find him in possession of a simple float. Grabbing on to one side, she waited while he did the same. They floated in the deep end,

adrift and alone. "You have to admit, this is the life."
She let out a satisfied sigh.

"Beats the daily grind, that's for sure." He slicked
back his dark hair.

"You said you're a writer."

He nodded. "I followed in the old man's footsteps."

She rested her chin against the plastic liner. "Do
you mind if I ask which father?"

He shook his head. "Ted Hou...my adoptive dad."
His voice took on an unmistakable warmth. "He's really the only father I have or care to recall. My real old
man took off, so there's not much point in remembering him."

"But you're close with your adoptive parents?"

"They're the best."

She smiled. "So are my parents. I think it's a wonderful gift when you can look back and know you've
had it good." She thought about her father, his
warmth, caring and the regular Sunday morning
breakfast with his "girls" as he called Juliette, Gillian
and their mother.

He'd given them so much love and acceptance—
which was probably why she felt so strongly about
protecting him now. "Do you ever feel you owe your
parents? Your adoptive parents, I mean, for giving
you more than a roof over your head?" Because her
parents had not only given her life but they'd sheltered her from the harsh realities of the press and
public scrutiny when they could, and they honestly

cared about her happiness. She sifted water through her hand, lost in thought.

"I know I owe them." At the sound of Doug's voice, she raised her head. "They saved me from the street." He cleared his throat.

"How so?"

"I was ten years old. I hadn't slept in days, unless you count resting on a park bench, and I hadn't eaten in twice as long. I was half a step away from foster care and one quarter step away from being arrested."

Hearing his story, her heart twisted at the pain no child should have to know. When she'd voiced her thoughts aloud, she'd been pondering how to save her father's reputation, not something as elemental as basic survival. Without thinking, she reached out and put her wet hand over Doug's arm, silently conveying her understanding.

His free hand covered hers. He glanced up, blinking into the sunlight, as if remembering. "Sometimes in the middle of the night, I'll wake up hungry and have to shake myself so I remember there's a full fridge downstairs and I'm not some ten-year-old kid out of options who has to resort to pickpocketing if I want food in my belly."

"I'm sorry," she said, feeling embarrassed at what seemed like shallower pursuits. "You know, when I asked you that question, I was thinking about my dad and how I can help him now. I never imagined..." She shook her head, not knowing what else to say. And even as she realized she'd mentioned her father, though not by name, she couldn't regret exchanging information with Doug. Not when he'd given her such insight into his past.

His blue eyes, reflecting and taking on the hue of the water, focused on her. "When you find yourself fortunate enough to have good parents and, believe me, I know the difference, there's little you wouldn't do in return. That's something I understand well."

Juliette nodded. He obviously could understand her desire to care for and protect the people who raised her.

"It sounds like you're here to sort something out. Something related to your dad?" He squeezed her hand, as if asking her to trust him.

"You could say that." She wondered what Doug would advise her if he knew the truth about who she was and what she'd been through. She wondered if her heart, which beat erratically in her chest and begged her to open up and let him in, could be trusted. After all, she'd made too many errors to be one-hundred-percent certain of her judgment and choices. But something inside her told her this man was different. That he wouldn't use her the way Stuart had. She'd already decided to trust him with her body. Her emotions couldn't possibly be far behind.

A loud whistle rent the air. "Beach volleyball," a woman's voice called out to the guests, breaking the opportunity to share and shattering the intensity between them. "Ten minutes until game time," the woman called once more.

Juliette forced a laugh, not knowing if she'd been spared or not. "Organized events." She shook her head. "They're for the people who can't stand to be idle."

"And people who like crowds," Doug muttered, seconds before ducking under the water for a quick escape.

Damned if Juliette hadn't done it again. She'd gotten him to open a vein and pour out his soul, when *he* was the one who needed information from her, not the other way around. But once he'd begun talking, he couldn't stop.

And he didn't understand why. He'd never revealed his painful past to anyone before, especially to a woman and, Lord knew, Erin would have lain prostrate at his feet for such in-depth information. Doug had had no desire to share with Erin, his girlfriend of two years, yet one day with Juliette and she knew his deepest secrets. Doug wasn't a fool and understood the kind of intimacy they'd just shared would go a long way toward gaining her trust and convincing her to open up in return.

He just wished his need for information on her ex-fiancé was the only reason he'd bared himself first. Wished he wasn't drawn to her compassionate nature and giving heart. Because he feared losing his own heart. And he hated the now constant guilt that accompanied his every move.

Doug resurfaced, shaking water off himself and

grabbing back on to the raft. "Volleyball interest you?" he asked.

"I know you said you wanted to try some resort activities, but I'm going to pass on the beach volleyball bit." She looked into his eyes and drew him in. "I prefer the company of one special person to a large group, myself."

Doug didn't miss her deliberate hint. And though beach volleyball was safer, he was too close to gaining her trust to push her away and risk losing her now. "I've got something special planned for us, remember?"

"Are you going to fill me in?"

He grinned. "Soon enough. For now all you need to do is head on back to your room. Everything you need for tonight will be waiting for you there."

"If I'm not careful, I could get used to this kind of attention."

"There's no reason why you shouldn't. A woman like you deserves the best." He reached forward with his feet, entangling their legs together beneath the water, and was rewarded by her huge smile.

His heart beat rapidly in his chest and he knew he was a goner. Hell, he should have known the minute he'd unburdened himself about his childhood. But with this one smile—meant for him alone—Doug knew he was falling for this woman fast and hard.

He hadn't lied when he'd told Merrilee he believed in happily ever after. He just hadn't thought any woman could inspire those kind of thoughts in him.

Least of all Juliette Stanton, the woman he needed for selfish reasons. He shook his head. Life had a way of throwing him the toughest curves.

He needed the information Juliette possessed too badly to walk away and he was mired too deep in lies to admit the truth outright and rely on her good nature for the answers. The guilt he'd been feeling since arriving at the island grew and settled in the pit of his stomach.

But so did his certainty that she was in possession of information he needed. Juliette had just admitted she'd come down here to sort out something related to her father. He wondered if Senator Stanton was involved with his protégé in illegal dealings and, though Doug would never dismiss the notion without evidence, he doubted it was true. His earlier information had never mentioned the senator and his record and reputation were above repute.

Which led Doug back to Juliette and her relationship with Stuart Barnes. Earlier this morning she'd questioned Doug about being engaged. She'd mentioned that by getting caught up in the swing of things, a person could end up nearly married. Without a doubt, she'd been talking about herself as well as about him.

So Juliette, of all people, would understand putting a parent first. Unfortunately she wouldn't appreciate being the one sacrificed for the cause. He thought of his father in ICU—the IV and other tubes poking and prodding him, and the smile on his weary face when

Doug had left to hunt down this story—and he knew one thing for sure. He didn't have a choice.

HOW DID HE KNOW? Juliette stood in front of the closet door that doubled as a full-length mirror, taking in the denim jeans, the white, oxford-type shirt with a tank top beneath, and the pair of simple black boots. All perfectly sized, all comfortable and easy. She wondered again how Doug could possibly know how badly she needed these ordinary clothes that symbolized an ordinary life.

She hadn't worn such a basic outfit since college and didn't have a pair of blue jeans in her wardrobe now. Ever conscious of public scrutiny, especially since she'd begun dating Stuart, she'd never left the house looking less than conservative and dressed up.

When the doorbell rang, she ran, intending to greet Doug with a huge hug of thanks. But as she twined her arms around his neck and his hands reached out to grasp her waist, simple gratitude became something more. Something primal and elemental, wild and free.

She tilted her head back, intending to just look at him, but the result put their bodies in intimate contact. His firm chest, covered by a denim shirt, pressed against hers, heightening the ache in her sensitive breasts. His belt buckle pushed into her stomach but that pressure was nothing compared to the hard outline of his erection snuggling against her femininity, a place where pressure built and desire found a home.

He sucked in a startled breath but didn't break their physical connection. "To what do I owe such an enthusiastic greeting?" he asked.

For a woman already on the edge, his grin was nothing short of devastating. "You anticipated my needs."

"How do you know that when you don't even know what I've got planned for tonight?"

"The jeans would have been enough."

He held on to her hand and twirled her out in front of him, letting out a whistle of approval. "Nice fit."

She felt the burn rise to her cheeks. He must have seen it because he stroked her heated skin with one roughened fingertip. "Never heard a catcall before?"

"Oh, I've heard them. I've just never had one directed at me."

His eyes darkened in appreciation. "Then the men in Chicago must be blind. Don't tell me a beautiful woman like you has never had a serious relationship."

She let out a sigh. Suddenly her recent past and the all's-well pretense here on the island became too heavy a burden. She wanted to share the truth. With Doug. "I probably came closer to getting married than you did."

His eyes narrowed. His interest was apparent but, by his furrowed eyebrows, so was his concern. "How close?" The words seemed reluctantly drawn from him. As if a part of him wanted to hear while another rebelled against it.

"Close enough to be wearing a wedding dress," she admitted softly.

Doug exhaled hard. He hadn't expected to get so much out of her so soon and hated the deception that caused her to open up to him now. He was using her fantasy and everything he knew she needed from a man to get information to help his cause—and yet there was nothing he'd done for her, nothing he would do, that was faked or phony. She was beautiful inside and out and irresistibly desirable too. He wanted nothing more than for her to believe it as well.

Even if she never gave him another piece of information about herself, her life or, damn him, her ex-fiancé, Doug would still be on this island fulfilling Juliette Stanton's fantasy. He just couldn't deny the benefits he might reap as a result.

"What kind of fool got that close to forever and let you get away?"

"The kind that has aspirations higher than he deserves." She shook her head and those loose curls spread over her shoulders. With a frustrated groan, she lifted the heavy mass of hair and pulled it back into a high ponytail, drawing his attention to her chiseled profile, defined cheekbones and full lips. "So what do you have planned for tonight?"

Her change of subject was obvious and Doug knew he had to accept the parameters. After all, she'd trusted him with so much more than he'd imagined possible after just one day.

He reached into his pocket and pulled out a red bandanna. "Does this give you a clue?"

She eyed the sheath of fabric with curiosity. "Not a one."

"I'm disappointed. Put the clothes together with the bandanna..."

She laughed. "Still nothing."

He shook his head. "Looks like you're going to have to humor me." He folded the scarf into a rectangular shape. "And trust me." Walking around her, he came up behind her and blindfolded her with the bandanna. "Now it's a real surprise."

Her hands reached upward and he playfully slapped them down.

"It's dark," she complained.

"That's the point. Hold my hand." Grasping her soft fingers in his, he walked her forward then helped her into the electric car he had waiting. He reached around to fasten her seat belt and caught a hint of her enticing, arousing scent. His body stiffened in response and he prayed for restraint. Then he placed her hands safely on the dashboard to steady her. "You okay?"

Her lips turned upward in a smile. "Dying of curiosity, but fine."

"Good. Anticipation's half the fun." He swung himself into the seat beside her. "Now hang on." He put the car in gear and drove them around the back of the resort and headed toward a secluded path, to the place Merrilee's staff had told him about earlier.

"We're here." He stopped the cart and shut off the motor.

Her nose crinkled upward and he realized she'd caught a whiff of their environment. "Any clue yet?"

"It smells like..." Before she could finish, he whipped off the bandanna, freeing her vision.

She blinked into the setting sunlight, adjusting to the shift in conditions before focusing on her surroundings.

"Horses! It smells like horse poop." She laughed. "This place is a stable! How amazing!" Grabbing on to the metal bar, she hauled herself out of the cart and jumped onto the ground. "I have always wanted to ride. When I was a little girl, I begged my father for a horse. He laughed and bought me a puppy instead. He was back and forth to Washington, D.C. too often to saddle himself or us with the responsibility of ponies, but I never stopped wanting one." Sheer joy edged her voice.

In her excitement, she hadn't even realized she'd connected her father to Washington, D.C. and opened the subject up for questioning. Doug knew. But any mention of her father would destroy the moment and he was too enthralled watching her happiness to burst her enthusiasm. And again, emotions won out over professional necessity. Doug stifled a curse, knowing this woman had him tied in knots in a way he'd never before experienced.

"I didn't know they had horses here."

"There isn't much Merrilee's missing."

She turned to face him. "So what's the plan?"

"An evening ride on the beach."

Her eyes opened wide and filled with gratitude. "I can't think of anything better."

Looking at her, neither could he. The stable hand privately warned Doug about an incoming tropical storm, common for this time of year, and the gray sky in the distance backed the claim. Doug promised to return early or take advantage of the shelter points set up along the route. The smart thing would be to give Juliette a brief ride and return quickly—but nothing about his reaction to Juliette, including his feelings, was smart. Still he'd been warned and the choice was his.

After touring the stables, they took off. The farther from the resort they traveled, the more pristine the beach, the whiter the sand and the farther they got from civilization. Because Doug had ridden before and the horse chosen for Juliette was gentle and easy, they'd gone out on their own, following the trail set by the staff. The ocean was choppy thanks to the incoming weather system and he kept the horses back from the tide.

Though Doug had planned this trip for Juliette, he was blown away by the beauty surrounding him and he wasn't just talking about the crashing waves, the endless deep blue water or even the dolphin he saw breaking through the surf. He was floored by Juliette's childlike reaction to the little things in life—like blue jeans and a horseback ride. And again, it was that innocence, in stark contrast to his jaded life, that beckoned to him.

He had much to learn from her, he realized, and glancing around he knew he was seeing the world for the first time—because her perspective was rubbing off on him. Changing him.

Thanks to the sound of the ocean and the noise made by the horses, they couldn't do more than drink in the serenity and relax to the steady beat of the hooves, and Doug was grateful. He couldn't speak if he wanted to. The lump in his throat was too great.

Dinner, some pointed questions and a quick return home—he reminded himself that was his plan. One that would minimize the risk to his heart, which he suspected was too far gone already. Finally they reached their destination on the other side of the island, and he transferred the horses to a stable hand.

"Where are we?" Juliette asked.

In response, he held out his hand and led her beyond the stables. Like much of Florida, this part of the island was decorated with pastel-colored stucco buildings, making the rougher city boy in him feel out of his element. He walked her toward a yellow house with lush tropical gardens he'd seen in the pictures this afternoon.

A birdbath with running water flowed freely out front. "This place is owned by a couple who used to work in a New York City restaurant and got tired of the pace. They hooked up with Merrilee, moved down here and they now cater to private parties," he explained.

"So it's just us?" He heard the hitch in her voice and understood the emotion because it obviously matched the feelings rioting inside him. His heart beat louder in his chest whenever she was near. The two of them alone was either a prelude to disaster or a trip to heaven in the making.

"I could call out the cavalry if you'd rather not be alone," he said lightly.

"There's no place else I'd rather be," Juliette said. And her body agreed.

She'd dreamed of riding a horse as a child, but never had she envisioned the adult feelings the powerful beast could stir. Sitting on the horse, her concentration on both the romantic scenery surrounding her and the incredible man by her side, she'd discovered the pounding surf had nothing on the pulse beating between her legs. The ride had taken on aphrodisiacal qualities and its effect hadn't lessened since she'd climbed down and into Doug's waiting arms.

Still strung tight from the vibration of riding the horse and thinking about Doug at the same time, she tingled in anticipation of them spending the evening alone. And two hours later, full from a lobster dinner and light-headed from a glass of wine, she still felt the same way. There hadn't been a lull in the conversation and they'd covered a broad range of topics, likes and dislikes, much like a first date.

She was more relaxed than she ought to be considering the intent way Doug studied her, yet she had no second thoughts about being with him, no hesitation or doubts that he was a good man.

"Are you ready to head back?"

She shook her head. "Are we in a rush? Because you wouldn't want me riding drunk would you?"

He laughed but she caught a hint of something that resembled anxiety in his. "I didn't realize one glass of wine over a two-hour dinner would hit you hard."

"Can I tell you a secret?" She folded her hands in front of her and leaned forward in her seat, then crooked her finger, indicating he should do the same.

He closed the distance, only a small table corner separating them, but before he could respond the waiter stopped by their table. "Excuse me, folks."

"Yes," Doug said through clenched teeth.

Well, at least he wasn't any happier with the intrusion than she was.

"I have a message from the main resort. There's a storm moving in faster than expected. The horses are in the stable and safe here but you'll have to take a car back. It's waiting out front, ready when you are."

"Thank you," Doug said. The waiter nodded and left them alone.

A storm. Juliette inhaled. Her fear of storms was juvenile and unreasonable, the result of a childhood foolishness that had left eight-year-old Juliette and Gillian stranded in a tree house in their backyard long after it was safe to be outdoors. Fear of being yelled at had been greater than their fear of rain, and by the time the girls realized the severity of the storm, thunder and lightning prevented their easy return. Her father had found them, finally, but not before lightning had struck a tree branch nearby and Juliette's fear of storms had been permanently instilled. Their parents' punishment had seemed mild in comparison.

Doug turned to face her. "See? We get a ride back. No drinking and riding issues at all."

She forced a smile and pushed her fear of storms away for now, in favor of Doug and more pressing concerns. "But there are other issues."

"Well, don't keep me in suspense."

She inclined her head. "It's not the wine that's hitting me hard but..." She drew in a deep breath for courage and strengthened the resolve she'd been developing throughout dinner.

She'd come so far in letting herself go. Another woman might not think so, but from her change in clothing to her outward flirting and the tingling awareness in her body, Juliette knew she'd taken great strides. Problem was, she hadn't gone as far as she would have liked, and she didn't want to have regrets when her time here was through.

Now that he'd given her not just a simple glimpse into his life but an overt revelation of childhood pain, she was comfortable with the man and knew she was ready. Ready to take that next step—the one Doug the gentleman had been obviously avoiding. Out of fear of offending her? She didn't know but it was time to find out.

He reached out and covered her hand. "But what?"

"It's you. You make me light-headed and dizzy. You affect me. And I was about to tell you I'm not ready to go home if it means leaving you standing at my doorstep again." She'd said it. Juliette let out a huge breath of air and waited.

Doug coughed, a sound that resembled a strangled groan and looked into her expectant gaze. The man who was attracted to her warred with the reporter who'd promised himself he wouldn't use her sexually to accomplish his goal. But, he reminded himself, he was also on this island to make her wishes come true. If he turned her away, he'd be crushing both her fantasy and her need to feel desired by that one special man. The man he'd set himself up to be. And the man who wanted her as much as she wanted him. Weighing the circumstances, he knew he could convince himself that being with her—at her request— wouldn't be using her for information.

But it was a thin argument. So he'd make damn sure she knew how badly he wanted her and make sure *she* enjoyed their intimacy. However, as he'd promised himself earlier, sleeping with her couldn't, wouldn't, happen.

He brushed his thumb back and forth over her soft skin before turning her palm up and grasping her hand in his. He rose, pulling her to her feet. "We should get going now, but we'll talk in the car on the way back."

She nodded.

He'd counted on a driver being a buffer for the sexual tension reverberating between them. Except the resort hadn't sent a shuttle van or a car as he'd expected. They'd sent a limousine, something he'd never have thought necessary on this small island resort. But, he realized, the limo, like the resort's owner, catered to people's fantasies. Recalling Merrilee questioning him about happily ever after, he knew the woman was a romantic. And what was more romantic than a limousine ride when necessary? The concept went all the way back to high school senior proms, he thought wryly.

This limo came complete with a shaded partition obliterating the driver's view of the passengers—and whatever behavior they chose to indulge in. And from the bright gleam in Juliette's eyes, the possibilities hadn't escaped her notice either.

But then she glanced at the darkening sky, thick now with gray clouds overhead. She shivered, a tremor shaking her hard. "Storms scare me," she whispered.

He raised an eyebrow in surprise.

"Old childhood fear. It's silly, I know." She squinted, studying the gray sky again.

"It wasn't supposed to roll in until later tonight."

She shrugged. "It happens." She climbed into the car and he followed.

The driver closed the door behind them and the rain began to fall—leaving Doug alone with a woman who looked like she'd jump into his lap at the first clap of thunder.

A woman he desired. Badly.

5

THUNDER CRACKLED overhead. Juliette clenched her hands tight in her lap. Lord, she was embarrassed. How could she seduce the man if she was too afraid to move? And she had no doubts she wanted to seduce Doug. None at all.

Without warning, his large hand covered hers. "Relax." He eased her hand out of its fist until her fingertips splayed—not across her thigh—but his. As a way to distract her, it worked. His leg was hard and strong beneath the rough denim and his powerful muscles flexed at her touch. She let out a slow exhale.

"You missed that last flash of lightning."

She met his amused gaze. "I had better things to think about."

He laughed. "That was the point."

A rumbling of thunder took her off guard. She tensed, curling her fingers around his leg. "Did you know if you count the seconds between the flash of light and the noise you can tell how far away the center of the storm is?"

"Truth or old wives' tale?" he asked.

"I don't know." Regardless, she'd stayed awake many nights focusing on the equation. "But thanks to you I've got something else to think about—at least during this storm." She lowered her voice, conveying a deliberate hint of mischief combined with desire.

His eyes darkened to a deep blue hue. "Whatever you've got in mind, will it keep you from being afraid?"

She nodded and shifted so she was facing him, then placed her hands on his shoulders. "I'll be way too preoccupied to even think about the weather." Juliette knew she was finding bravery in the darkened car, courage in his physical and emotional strength.

"Then by all means let's keep you distracted." His husky voice sent awareness shooting through her veins.

The storm, her nerves and overwhelming need had her trembling. With shaking hands, she moved her fingers to the buttons on his shirt. Two buttons were already opened and her fingers brushed the coarse hair on his chest. He sucked in a breath of air and when he let it out, the sound came out a ragged groan. One Juliette felt deep in her belly and lower, in the pulsing place between her legs.

Power. He'd just proven she possessed the power to affect a man physically, something she'd seriously doubted. Doug might not realize the importance of her discovery but she'd never forget this gift, this moment or this man.

She slipped the tiny white button through the buttonhole and repeated the motion with the next, then the next. All the while his heated breath whispered against her cheek and she inhaled his seductive, masculine scent with each intake of air. And a tiny moan of need escaped her throat.

Doug leaned his head back against the seat and shut his eyes tight. She was killing him by degrees—her delicate, hesitant touches, her wide-eyed stare, and her ability to put fear aside and get lost in her gentle exploration of him. He was fulfilling her fantasy and giving her back the heady power of awareness and desire, but he was also discovering he had needs of his own.

He opened his eyes when, as if she'd read his mind, she parted his shirt, pushing the garment off his shoulders, baring his chest to her gaze. Her hands tangled in his chest hair, her fingertips brushed his nipples and her lips caressed his sensitized flesh until he shook with unrestrained need.

Lightning flashed in the sky and thunder crashed around them. By the formula she'd explained earlier, they were now in the center of the raging storm. But Juliette was too consumed, creating a storm of her own, to notice. And he was too lost in her fragrant scent and the incredible sensation she created in his body to point it out. Getting lost himself wasn't what he'd had in mind when he'd set out to ease her fear and soothe her nerves. His heart galloped faster than the horse he'd ridden earlier and desire pulsed deep inside. Strung tight, he was the one that needed calming now and he wouldn't find the relief he sought if she continued her sensual moves.

With her damp tongue, she licked a path up his chest, lingering on his neck, and pausing when she reached his ear. "I'm distracted," she whispered in a soft voice with husky undertones.

"I'm sure you are." He placed his hands safely at his sides. For one thing, he'd promised himself he wouldn't get involved *this* way and for another she was doing a fine job of distracting herself from her fear of storms.

She didn't need his hands on her body, or his mouth on her lips... He clenched his teeth at the erotic, arousing, *tempting* possibilities.

"Am I distracting you?" She bit down lightly on his earlobe, sending him soaring to even greater heights of heaven and hell.

"We're here, folks." The driver's voice sounded from the intercom system in the car. "Juliette's stop is first."

Somehow Doug was aware enough to realize the driver hadn't given away Juliette's last name. He'd protected her anonymity, a reminder to Doug of where he was and what he was doing. Or shouldn't be doing, he thought wryly. The return to the resort had come just in time.

The car came to a stop but the driver didn't get out to help them from the car. He was obviously giving Doug and Juliette a chance to talk. A chance Doug had forgotten about earlier in favor of helping her through her fear and enjoying her gentle but heated touches.

"I guess this is it," Doug said.

She lifted his shirt back onto his shoulders, a mischievous grin on her lips. "It doesn't have to be. Remember what I said before. I don't want to go inside and leave you standing at my doorstep again." Her words were strong but the tremor in her voice revealed her vulnerability.

"You wouldn't be leaving me on your doorstep this time. I'd be in a dry car." He spoke lightly, feeling anything but.

No matter how much she desired him, she'd run the other way if she knew he was the man who'd broken the story about her ex-fiancé's partner. He wanted to give her her fantasy, but he needed to respect himself more.

He started to close his shirt buttons, needing the distraction, but she swatted his hands away and handled the chore herself—forcing him to watch her bent head as she worked, letting him drink in the sight and scent of the riotous head of curls she'd freed earlier.

She finished and rested her hands in her lap. "A real gentlemen would walk me to my door. And once he got there, would he really want to let me go in alone?"

Yes. No. What *he* wanted didn't matter and Doug knew damn well he was no gentleman.

Another flash lit up the dark sky. Her wide, bright eyes shone with hope, asking him not to let her down. Thunder immediately followed and Doug knew he was doomed. No way would he send her inside to face the rest of the storm and the rest of the night alone. He wondered if fate was laughing as it prevented him from doing the noble thing. Doug had never considered himself honorable yet when it came to Juliette, he didn't recognize the man he'd become.

In answer to her question, he pushed open the door and stepped out into the rain. He wasn't surprised when the driver practically materialized by his side or when Juliette hesitated at the edge of the car's back seat to stare up at the stormy sky.

"You took long enough to decide. I don't mind being alone. I'm an adult, no matter how foolish I've acted, and I've survived many thunderstorms on my own."

He held out his hand but she stubbornly refused to grasp it. "Are you waiting until I drown?" he asked.

She set her jaw tight. "I don't want you coming with me out of pity."

He reached forward and grabbed her hand, hauling her out of the car and into his arms. Ignoring the driver and the rain, he pulled her flush against him. "Does this feel like I pity you?" He whispered the words, harsh and as desperate as he felt, in her ear.

Her eyes opened wide.

"I don't know why you're surprised. Thanks to that distraction you needed, you've spent the last half hour gearing me up."

"You're certainly feeling aroused."

"By *you*."

"You don't say?" She grinned and he couldn't help but kiss the smile on those damp lips.

She laughed and kissed him back, twining her arms around his neck and opening her mouth, letting him deep inside. Somewhere beside him he heard the gunning of the car motor and knew the driver had left them behind.

Grasping her hand, he pulled her beneath the portico of her cottage. The overhang was small and barely granted them coverage. "We should get inside."

She licked at the water on her lips. "We should and we could—but then I'd never get over my fear of storms. But if we were to replace the bad memories with something wonderful." Her voice trailed off. Deliberately provocative, husky and sure.

"Then we'd have a cure for phobias. We could market it and make millions."

She laughed. "I'm game if you are."

He groaned, conceding defeat. He was here and unless he wanted to walk back to the main resort and his room in the rain, he wasn't going anywhere anytime soon. Nor could he back off without giving her the wrong impression and making her unsure and vulnerable, two things he never wanted her to be again. Especially not when she was with him.

"What the hell," he muttered and sealed his lips tight against hers.

Though he knew he couldn't justify this with the notion that he was fulfilling her fantasy, at the moment, he didn't care—about anything except feeling and tasting the erotic mixture of rainwater and Juliette. He stroked her lips with his tongue and delved into the deep recesses of her mouth, learning and giving one minute, devouring then gentling the next.

The rumble of thunder, when it came, was softer than before but she still stiffened. "Easy."

Her muscles slackened and he ran his hands up and down her arms, warming her through her damp shirt and attempting to heat her body with the same fire raging through him. But a chill shook her slender frame and Doug knew their time outdoors was coming to an end. Something he couldn't allow until he'd done as she asked and replaced her old fear of storms with a new kind of awareness—a tempest of arousal and emotion that culminated in blinding ecstasy. One she wouldn't forget or ever fear.

With that thought, he slipped his hand between them, cupping her intimately, waiting for a signal of rejection or acceptance, knowing he'd heed either. But when his hand found a warm, welcoming home in the juncture of her thighs, he hoped like hell she wouldn't have second thoughts now.

She let out a whimper of assent, a soft mew of satisfaction, and just when he thought he'd been granted his deepest desire, she shifted her stance, parting her legs and affording him greater access. He'd wanted her permission. He'd received her submission instead. Her complete and utter trust, he thought, and an alien emotion rose in his chest—something tender and warm, pushing hard into his throat and nearly stopping his breath. The feelings she inspired should have sent him running, but he was beyond reason. Beyond anything except this woman and this moment.

Juliette sighed, tingling with anticipation. He flattened his palm against her *there* and despite the heavy barrier of denim, his fingers managed to dip inward, creating a rising tide of emotion she'd never experienced before. She shuddered and grabbed for his shoulders, certain she'd fall without support.

So *this* was what real desire felt like. Swirling sensations that kept her light-headed and dizzy. A relentless tugging that caused her heart to pound, her throat to close, and made that delicious pulling sensation he created between her thighs not close to being enough.

He brushed her damp hair off her face with one hand. "Where are you now?"

A warm smile lifted her lips. "I'm drowning in...desire." She'd nearly said emotion before catching herself with a mental warning. *Don't rush things*, she silently cautioned but feared she was falling hard anyway.

"Not fear?"

"Is there anything to be afraid of?" she asked immediately, catching her own dual meaning.

As if testing her, the elements chose that moment to make themselves known. Though the sky didn't illuminate with light, thunder rumbled overhead. Her fingers curled into his shoulders but she knew she was safe.

He grasped her chin in his hand and turned her to him. "Not with me. You never have to fear me."

And looking into those gorgeous blue eyes, she believed. Without warning, he shifted her attention from his face to herself by rocking his other hand against her body, and the place he owned with his masterful touch. Warmth, heat and intense sensation collided, bringing her to the brink of release faster than she'd ever dreamed possible.

"Where are you?" he asked her again, rotating his palm against her mound, pressing deep with his fingertips, playing her hard and well.

Unable to speak, she swallowed a moan and he released the exquisite building pressure, stopping her assent. "Doug, please." Her hips jerked forward in a silent plea.

"Just tell me where you are," he said, his own voice gruff with desire and raw emotion. "Open your eyes and look around."

Had she closed them? Juliette forced her eyelids open and glanced over her shoulder into the dark night. "I'm outside."

He rewarded her answer with just the right movement of his hand, the perfect rotation of his palm and fingertips, keeping the momentum going until she knew she was riding that wave once more, but stronger this time.

Holding on to Doug for support, she leaned her

head backward, jerking her hips forward at the same time, seeking harder, deeper pressure.

"Is it raining?" he asked.

Knowing the result if she ignored the question in favor of sensation, she blinked and forced the answer from inside her. "Yes."

He'd found the perfect turning, twisting motion and his hand seemed connected to her body, bringing her closer and closer to...

"Lightning?" he asked.

She was so, so near... Her body shook and a yawning emptiness warred with the cataclysmic fulfillment that was almost within reach. She didn't want to speak, she wanted to *feel*. "No, no lightning. Not anymore."

He quickly shifted their positions, leaning her against the door and repositioning his hand. The door gave her more solid support against her back, letting him thrust as hard and deep as he could, pushing her to the outer limits of desire.

"Thunder?" His voice sounded as hoarse and raw as she felt.

"Yes." The pulsing picked up momentum and her hips gyrated against his hand. "Oh, yes."

"What are you going to think of next time it rains?" His voice rasped in her ear.

"You," she said as her body exploded.

He sealed his lips over hers, catching the word in his mouth, joining with her for the first wave of blinding light that could have been lightning striking them and she wouldn't have cared.

Then the languorous, incredible waves subsided and reality set in. She'd come on to this man in a way that was completely foreign to her and she'd experienced delight at his hands. Much as she'd enjoyed it, she was mortified and didn't know how she'd face him now.

"COFFEE'S READY." Juliette walked into the sitting area of the small cottage holding two white mugs.

She wore a silky two-piece outfit that covered more skin than Doug would have liked, yet teased him with a low dip in the neckline and a faint outline of her full curves. Curves he'd still like to feel thoroughly and without the barrier of clothes.

He cleared his throat. "Thank you. Hot coffee's great."

"Are you still chilled?" She set the drinks on the table in front of the couch.

Though she'd been able to change into dry clothes, he'd had no choice but to remain in his damp ones. The jeans weren't too wet but his shirt had soaked through, so he'd taken it off and wrapped a towel around his neck for comfort.

He picked up the mug, letting the heat pass from the cup through his body. "I'm better now." Not because of the coffee but thanks to his view of Juliette.

Her hair fell in soft curls over her shoulders, her skin was makeup free and she turned him on more than any woman he'd seen dressed for a night on the town.

"This place amazes me. It's got all the comforts of home and yet I've never felt further from my life." She shifted her legs from one position to the next, while twisting one long lock of hair around her finger.

"I don't feel much closer to mine," he muttered. A chill shook him—from the rain, or her effect on him, he didn't know.

"I wish I had something warmer for you to wear but I barely recognize the clothes in my suitcase and, trust me, there's nothing remotely big enough to fit you."

She couldn't look him in the eye—or anywhere else for that matter. Doug wondered if he'd ever known a truly modest woman before. He wished she wasn't so uncomfortable about the incredible experience they'd just shared. He wished he had a dry shirt to put on and ease her discomfort. But a bigger part of him wanted her comfortable with him, undressed or not. And damned if he didn't want to repeat their outdoor experience, but this time they'd be in a warm bed and he'd be inside her body.

He swiped a weary hand over his eyes. Now that couldn't happen. He'd already taken things further than he'd ever dreamed and, besides, her fidgeting told him how ill at ease she truly was.

The only way to distract himself from the impossible was talk. "Did you buy all new clothes for this trip?" he asked, picking up on her comment about barely recognizing the clothes in her suitcase.

"Not hardly." Her laugh had a wry sound and he suddenly wondered if she was sitting before him wearing honeymoon clothes. Wondering if her skimpy bathing suits and sexy lounging wear had been meant for a different trip. For another man's devouring gaze.

His stomach cramped at the thought of another male viewing her at all. Whether she was sexy in her navy two-piece suit or disheveled from a run in the rain, Doug wanted to be the only man who witnessed all the various facets of Juliette Stanton. Damn. Where the hell had these proprietary feelings come from and how did he get rid of them?

He glanced up just as she ran her tongue over her bottom lip. "My sister surprised me with this trip," she admitted, "and with the wardrobe."

Relief, pure and sweet, flooded his veins. In an indirect way, her clothing was meant for him alone. "Your sister sounds incredible."

Juliette nodded. "She is special. We're twins actually. What about you? Any brothers or sisters?"

He shook his head. "My parents couldn't have kids, which is why they took me in so easily." And though he'd be forever grateful, he'd often wondered what it would be like to have a brother or sister. Someone close to his own age to look out for him when times were tough and slap him on the back when things were good. "Did you and your sister always get along?"

She nodded. "She's my best friend. She gets me through the worst of times."

Hearing her refer to her recent past and divulge facts he already knew, his stomach clenched again. How many times in the past had someone bared their soul and he'd devoured the information without reservation? If he'd had qualms, he'd justified them with the notion of just doing his job. So he thought he'd been, if not prepared, then at least aware of how he'd feel gaining information from Juliette.

But from the beginning, his dealings with Juliette had been different. Guilt had been his companion, one he didn't recognize but had grown used to. And it made Doug feel sick.

He forced a grin. "So there are two of you." He caught his choice of words and shook his head, needing to rephrase. "You may be twins but you're too unique to be alike. Too special." And that truth wasn't forced.

"Thanks." Gratitude filled her eyes and she finally met his gaze. "Gillian, my sister, she's more outgoing, so much less reserved." Her voice trailed off and Doug knew she'd just recalled their time in the storm. Her lashes fluttered, her stare shifted and a faint blush stained her cheeks.

"Hey." He reached out and touched her chin, giving her no choice but to look him head-on. "What happened between us? It was supposed to give you good memories to replace the bad ones, not make you too embarrassed to be with me."

Her flush deepened. "It's just that..."

"Say it." He pushed her, curious to hear what caused her discomfort and withdrawal.

She let out a breath of air. "It's like I asked and you provided. And you got nothing in return."

Did she really have no idea? He'd been so affected by her orgasm he'd nearly come just watching. He'd never reacted so strongly to a woman before, never cared so much about someone else's pleasure, his own be damned.

And the one thing he knew without question was the feelings crowding inside him and begging for release weren't going to be easily controlled. "That's not the way I remember it."

"You're telling me it wasn't one-sided?"

It was time for a revelation of his own. "We both have our fantasies, Juliette." What had he said to Merrilee? *I need to know I can put a woman before myself.*

At the time it had been a line to get him in the door and pair him with Juliette, though admittedly the words had held some truth. But in kissing, caressing and giving to this woman, Doug *had* learned—not only that it was possible to put her first physically, but that he wanted to put her first emotionally as well.

She leaned forward, ready to listen.

And he was ready to tell her. He hadn't expected to reveal his fantasy to Juliette, but she made him want to open up and share. "I recently hurt someone I cared about. I hurt her badly. From her perspective, I was using her and I suppose she wasn't far from wrong. So now I want to prove I can put a woman's needs before my own."

Curious green eyes met his. "And will just any woman do?"

"No way." He shook his head. "And no way are you just *any* woman. Not to me."

She splayed her hands on her thigh, fingering the silken material. "But you can't deny things were one-sided. And I have to know—was it because you were using me to prove a point?"

"No more than I assume you're using me for reasons relating to your own fantasy." He laughed. "You are a stubborn one. Technically, yes, it was one-sided. But..." He paused deliberately.

Long enough for her curiosity to win out and for her to glance up. "But what?"

Doug leaned forward until they were inches apart. "But..." He reached for her hand. "You've come to mean a lot to me in a very short time. And I enjoyed watching you. And I enjoyed listening to you. Did you know you make these little sounds? Sighs, gasps, moans of pleasure?"

Her pupils dilated. A flush spread from her neck up her cheeks. Her mouth opened in a small O then closed without making a sound. Heat flooded his system and he broke into a sweat. In reassuring her, he was arousing himself all over again.

It was probably his punishment and penance. To be so close to the woman he desired and know he had to keep his distance, for her sake as well as his own. Because to make *his* fantasy come true—to be able to look himself in the mirror and to see he could put a woman, *this* woman, before himself—he couldn't go further. Couldn't sleep with her. Even if doing so would fulfill a fantasy of another kind, his conscience and soul were at risk. And so was his heart.

But he forced himself to concentrate on her needs. "And those sounds?" He drew both himself and her back to the point at hand.

"Yes?" The word came out a barely audible gasp.

"They turn me on."

Juliette swallowed hard. He was doing it again, she thought, dazedly. Soothing her. Easing one kind of distress while creating a new one of an entirely different sort. He was so obviously setting out to convince her that her pleasure had been his as well.

And he was convincing. Enough to relax her and loosen her inhibitions again. To remind her that as much as he needed to prove to himself he was a decent person and could put someone else's needs first, she'd promised herself something as well—that she'd take this one week to break free and be herself. That she'd experiment, with no constraints, problems or reporters to hinder her inhibitions.

She'd trusted Doug to give her ultimate pleasure once before. Modesty and shyness wouldn't help either of them now. "Doug?"

"Yes?"

She grasped on to the short length of time they had left on the island—the time they had left together—and marshaled the courage she needed. "Are you still turned on?"

He sucked in a deep breath of air. The "yes" came out in a drawn-out hiss, one he couldn't hold back, though he'd obviously tried. She'd take it as an affirmative answer.

Grasping on to the ends of the white towel, she pulled him close. She inhaled his potent, masculine scent, and her body, already on the edge, reacted. Her nipples tightened and desire coiled deep in her belly—both familiar and welcome reactions to this man.

Familiar. In a short time he'd become more familiar and endearing than her ex-fiancé ever had been. Why had she been willing to settle for less? "Let me take care of you this time."

She spoke the words at the same time she covered his mouth with her own, using the movement of her lips and the vibration of speech to make her point. To arouse him with her words and her touch, just as he'd done to her.

His hands gripped her shoulders and she felt his indecision in the way he kept the kiss light and his hold on her firm, preventing their bodies from touching intimately. Just because Juliette now knew what caused his hesitation didn't mean she'd allow him to turn her away. Testing her feminine wiles, testing him, she teased his lips with a light flicker of her tongue.

She obviously made her point because his heartfelt groan resulted in a change—their kiss became the deepest, sweetest one she'd ever known. Juliette figured she'd made headway. And when he matched her move, dipped into her mouth with his tongue, she stopped thinking at all.

6

SWEET HEAVEN. And that's where he was. Losing himself in her warm, wet, willing mouth once more. Warning bells were ringing hard, but he couldn't bring himself to heed them. Doug didn't break the kiss as his hands slid from her shoulders and around her back, settling on her waist. Barriers, even silken ones, were no longer acceptable and he lifted the flowing material so he could caress her soft skin.

She stopped him with a firm grip on his wrists. "Your turn, remember?"

Her voice broke through the haze of desire, bringing him back to reality. He didn't want anything from her.

He swallowed a curse. He might lie to her but he wouldn't lie to himself. He wanted anything and everything she had to give. He just couldn't let himself take. "I told you I didn't expect anything in return." His voice sounded rough to his own ears.

"I know that. You gave because you wanted to, even if you were proving a point to yourself. Now *I* want to give back." She drew a deep breath, one Doug knew for certain was for courage, and then placed her hand on the front placket of his jeans.

He gritted his teeth. She must have sensed his aching need because she cupped him more firmly and slid her palm down then up again in an excruciatingly slow but tantalizing movement. Certainty combined with endearing hesitancy showed in her face as she felt, tested and learned his shape and contours. His body came alive beneath her touch and he barely held himself in check.

"Are you going to deny you like that?" she asked.

He couldn't admit or deny. Need and arousal collided inside him, fast and intense. "I think the hard evidence speaks for itself."

She laughed, the sound light and easy, despite their serious conversation and the fact that they were both on the edge. But when she reached for the button on his jeans, Doug knew he had to call a stop. Now, before things went too far. But he also knew he'd be hurting her if he turned her away.

Although he'd explained his fantasy, she was still vulnerable and she'd never completely understand why he stopped so soon. Considering how badly he wanted her, he was having a hard time understanding it himself—and he was in possession of the facts.

Holding back, not taking what she offered and losing himself inside her willing body—Doug didn't recognize the man making the sacrifice. He hadn't done many things in his life to be proud of, Doug thought. Obtaining and printing facts by any means possible, even if they revealed others' failings, hardly qualified him for sainthood.

Yet here he was, denying himself what he wanted most, what he wanted even more than the information she possessed, because it was best for Juliette.

She was new and special and brought something good into his life. In an ironic way, he owed her for that, Doug thought. And this was the only way he could repay her.

She flipped open the button on his jeans and her fingers grabbed the zipper next. He inhaled, wondering how to stop her.

"Remember I told you I was engaged?" Her voice and the topic she chose took him by surprise, but he managed a nod.

"What I didn't tell you was there were no sparks." She released his fly and the rasping sound echoed in his ears.

He clenched his fists at his sides.

"No excitement." Her hands went to the waistband on his jeans. "No real desire."

She paused—thank God—because he needed to hear everything she said, words as well as inflection, and he couldn't do that if she was undressing him. And he couldn't stop her or the topic of conversation would turn and he'd never get this insight into Juliette.

Insight he wanted for personal, not professional, reasons. No agenda involved. He wanted to hear what she had to say because he needed to know the source of her pain. And he wanted to make it go away. Not because it was his so-called fantasy, but because he was on the verge himself.

On the verge of falling for her, hard, deep and fast. A first he had no clue how to handle. "I can't imagine any man not wanting you." He spoke, Doug realized, with his heart. And that particular organ began to pound harder inside his chest.

She bit down on her lower lip. "Then don't imagine it, just trust me. He didn't want me. And I thought it was my fault," she said softly. "I'd been through something similar once before and it just reinforced the feelings. A man couldn't want me, just what I could give him or do for him."

Doug's journalistic instincts kicked in, telling him he was seconds away from the truth. She could very well admit her secrets, yet the adrenaline flowing through his system had nothing to do with his ultimate goal and everything to do with her distant, hurt expression.

He touched her cheek. "You have to know I want you."

"I do." A smile lifted her lips and lightened her eyes. An honest, grateful, trusting kind of smile. "And since we're admitting fantasies, you have to know you've been fulfilling mine. And it's been an incredible gift."

"How's that?"

"You've given me back my faith in myself," she said simply. Without warning, she refocused on her original task and grabbed onto the waistband of his jeans.

He had seconds to make a choice. Doug wasn't an indecisive man. He went after his goals, consequences be damned. Hell, the newspaper article and his busted career were proof of that. But when it came to Juliette Stanton, all his intentions and resolutions to go no further were constantly shot to hell the minute she came within touching distance. Kissing distance. Any distance.

He grasped her wrists, stilling their determined movements and giving himself something to do with his restless hands—hands that would rather be roaming her supple curves. "If I've restored your faith in yourself, does that mean you believe in me?"

"Of course."

That simple, he thought. And that complicated. "And you believe I want you."

She nodded. A light blush stained her cheeks as she gestured with a tip of her head. "Hard evidence, like you said."

Twining their hands together, he eased himself closer, so he could cradle her in his arms and resist temptation at the same time. "Then can you believe that I want to know you better more than I..." he cleared his throat, "want you to reciprocate. Right now, anyway."

"I can believe in you enough to trust what you say." Juliette rested her head against his chest.

Closing her eyes, she could see his face behind her

shut lids. If she'd thought him handsome earlier this evening, after a run in the rain and her fingers in his hair, he was devastating and her pulse rate increased rapidly.

"You should. Remember I'm not the one with the fear of storms. If I didn't want to be here, I could walk out the door."

What he said made sense. Of course he could walk away. And unlike the past men in her life he didn't know who she was, therefore he couldn't want anything from her except sex or her company. Phrased that way, she ought to be grateful he'd opted to get to know her better first, she realized, and she let herself relax against him, trusting him even more.

After all, no man had ever shown interest in *her*. Doug did. And her interest wasn't just reciprocated, it ran high. But he was holding himself in check and Juliette had no doubt his restraint was related to his fantasy. He wanted to prove he could put a woman's needs first, before his own. Unfortunately, that put his fantasy at odds with her desire.

She'd already experienced the luxury of being catered to and doted upon by a very special man. With Doug, she felt desirable and the center of his universe. At times she even forgot the hurt of her broken engagement. And now that Doug had completed her basic fantasy—one she hadn't known she'd possessed before coming down to this island—she wanted more.

But first she had to prove to him they could share

more intimacy and make love without one or the other of them being used for selfish gain.

He said he wanted to get to know her better. It was a start toward her goal and she had no problem complying. "So what is it you want to know about me?"

"How about we begin with your fear of storms."

She curled into his waiting strength. His arms cocooned her in safety and heat but she couldn't ignore the tingling awareness rioting through her. "Dad built us a tree house when we were eight. It was so cool and Gillian and I spent so much time there. Too much time, so Mom and Dad had to restrict the hours. But we were kids, you know? We just had to play there no matter what."

"And here I thought you were the perfect child."

She shook her head. "Gillian was the wild child, which made me the *more* perfect daughter, but that came later, as I got older. At eight I just wanted to have fun."

"Nothing wrong with having fun." He rested his chin on her head and Juliette sighed.

The comfort and ease of the situation wasn't lost on her. Not only did he understand, he was interested. He cared. "I liked fun too. We were playing at Stuart's house..."

"Stuart?" he asked.

"My...neighbor. Fiancé," she admitted, not wanting to bring the word into her private time with Doug but wanting honesty between them just the same. He let out a low growl but before he could question her about Stuart the man, she continued her childhood story. "And it was getting late. When it started to drizzle, his parents sent us home."

Doug groaned. "Let me guess. You detoured."

"Right. And then it started to pour."

"Aha." His drawn-out word rumbled deep in his chest.

"Exactly. By the time Gillian and I heard the rain, it was so late we were afraid to go back. At eight years old, punishment is scary. We spent too long arguing over what to do and, before you know it, thunder, lightning and major windswept rain was coming down. We were soaked, scared and wanted to go home." She shook her head, remembering. "Dad found us first."

"Of course he did. You guys were in the most obvious place to look."

She laughed. "I said we were eight years old. I didn't say we were smart. But he found us after lightning hit a branch on a neighboring tree. I don't think I've ever been so scared. I was holding on to Gillian and crying, while she was having the adventure of a lifetime." She shrugged. "And that's why I'm afraid of storms. I guess I should have known then I wasn't cut out for too much excitement."

"Oh, I think you handle excitement extremely well."

There was that deep rumble again, Juliette thought. The sexy sound that reverberated inside her, turning her inside out and making her want him even more than she already did. "Depends on who's sharing the excitement with me."

"Right now that would be me."

She rested her head against his shoulder. "You won't get any argument from me." She stretched her feet out on the couch and he followed suit. Though cramped, she'd never felt more at ease.

Perhaps because he'd freed them from jumping into anything immediately sexual, he'd taken the pressure off. Thanks to Stuart, she possessed this driving need to entice a man and prove he could be interested. Thanks to Doug there wasn't another man who interested her except for him. He'd just shown her a nonphysical but still intimate way of expressing that interest. And she was grateful. Enough to let herself go and relax in his arms, the rain outside distant and so far away.

SHE WAS BEING shifted, lifted and carried. She hadn't realized she'd fallen asleep but Juliette awoke with a start to find herself held in Doug's arms. "What are you doing?"

"Moving before I wake up permanently twisted like a pretzel."

She laughed. "You could have just woken me."

"And miss the opportunity to hold you in my arms? Not a chance."

He carried her into the bedroom and deposited her on the bed, going so far as to pull down the covers and tuck her in, then lower himself onto the mattress beside her. Such a parental gesture, yet there was nothing familial about the heat in Doug's eyes or the sizzling awareness he ignited inside her. Her pulse rate kicked into overtime as she waited for whatever he had to say.

He picked up a lock of her hair, twisting a long strand around his fingertip, seemingly distracted, but Juliette knew better. He was savoring every touch, every feel, just as she did whenever he was near. She curled into the downy softness of the pillows beneath her.

"Rain's stopped," he murmured.

"You're leaving." Unexpected, unreasonable disappointment filled her.

"I don't have a choice." His gaze fell from her face to the low neckline on her shirt. His fingers followed the movement, tracing the straight edging from her collarbone downward, brushing her chest and lingering in the deep vee nestled between her breasts.

His tanned skin contrasted with her paler flesh and though his touch was gentle, his intent was sexual. And Juliette experienced an instant flare of heat. Suddenly the silk top, which had been so soft seconds earlier, rasped against her hardened nipples. Nothing would ease the tension inside her except his touch, and from the determined look in his eyes, that wouldn't be happening now.

Let loose. Be yourself. What other way to break past his stubborn convictions? "Of course you have a choice. You can stay."

His jaw clenched tight. "Not yet."

She wanted to question him further, find out what kind of hurt he believed he'd inflicted in the past or why he felt the need to atone now. "Why..."

Before she could finish, he dipped his head and lowered his lips to hers for another one of his long, drugging kisses. The kind that sapped her energy and stopped all rational thought. And the kind that told her whatever reason he wasn't staying the night had nothing to do with his feelings for her.

While he worked magic with his mouth, his fingertips eased inside her shirt and though he encountered the barrier of her flimsy bra, he wasn't deterred. With a light touch, he held her nipple between two fingers, rolling and flicking with enough pressure to first ease the ache and then increase it.

She raised her arms, seeking to touch him, too, but he gripped her hands and held them against the mattress, keeping himself in charge. And her at his mercy. She sighed into him, letting him know with her mouth, the only way she could, how much she enjoyed his ministrations and how badly she wanted more.

"I don't want to go." He leaned his forehead against hers.

His admission sent talons of hope soaring through her veins. "Then don't."

"You've been hurt recently."

She stiffened at the reminder. "I never said that."

"Your ex-fiancé wanted what you could do for him and not you. I'd call that hurt."

"And you ought to know?" She deliberately pressed harder.

"Something like that."

Accepting his vague answer for now, she stored further questions away for another time.

He lifted her chin in his hand. "If I stay, we both know where this is headed."

She nodded, her heart filling with heated warmth.

"But for your sake you need to be sure."

"I think I know what my body is telling me." And right now it was screaming for his touch.

He laughed but didn't sound at all amused. "I want your mind to know it, too. And that takes time."

More like *he* needed time, Juliette thought. As difficult as it was, she heeded his boundaries but Juliette didn't plan on leaving the island without breaking past his barriers and experiencing complete intimacy—his body, deep inside hers. She trembled at the thought of making love with Doug, knowing she'd never be the same afterward.

He lifted the covers and tucked them around her, then leaned forward for another brief kiss. "Night."

She sighed. Knowing what was right and necessary didn't make saying goodbye any easier.

WHEN THE TELEPHONE rang, Juliette was in another world. Alone with Doug on a deserted island, surrounded by bright sun and tropical flowers with the softest petals—for which Doug found the most inventive, arousing uses. She didn't want to be disturbed, but the persistent ringing wouldn't abate.

Reaching over, she grabbed the receiver. "Hello." If she had to be awakened, she hoped it would be by Doug.

"When I sent you on this trip I didn't think you'd forget to check in. How are you?" Gillian's concerned voice came through loud and clear.

"There aren't supposed to be phones in paradise," Juliette wailed. But she couldn't deny she was happy to hear from her sister even if the feminine voice wasn't her first choice.

She closed her eyes, but her dream slipped further and further from her grasp, replaced by reality: a too-cold room courtesy of the air conditioner, a too-cold bed thanks to Doug's late-night departure and a humming, lingering emptiness because her dream had stopped short of satisfaction.

"If you're in paradise, why do you sound so miserable?" Gillian asked.

"Not miserable." Lonely for the man who'd left too quickly last evening. Juliette sat up in bed, letting the morning sun stream through the blinds and bathe her in warmth. "And I recall leaving a message on your answering machine the day I got down here."

Gillian cleared her throat. "Yes, well, would you believe I was out and too busy to get back to you?"

"Too afraid is more like it. I know you, Gillian Stanton. You were afraid to hear what I had to say about you arranging a *fantasy* vacation without telling me—oh, and switching my wardrobe. You knew I'd have a few choice words on that subject, too."

"When I didn't hear back from you again I got worried."

She wasn't surprised her sister had all but ignored the issue at hand. "You should be worried," Juliette muttered. "It would serve you right."

"That bad an idea?"

She didn't miss the hesitancy in Gillian's voice and decided she'd tortured her sister enough. Besides, she needed her twin and best friend's advice. "It was probably the best idea you've had in this lifetime," she admitted.

"Wow! That good. Well, I read about Fantasies, Inc. in a magazine. Would you believe couples actually end up *married* thanks to that resort and its owner?"

Married. Before Juliette could either process the word or speak, Gillian continued. "And speaking of married—or more accurately, not married—you should know Stuart's been suspiciously silent since you've been gone."

Juliette let out a stream of breath. "Silent in what way? I haven't been in contact with him since we came to that so-called understanding to keep quiet."

"He called the day you left."

"He called *me*?" Gillian was staying in Juliette's house to throw the reporters off the trail. "Why would Stuart want to deal with me now?"

"Most likely he was checking up on you and, believe me, he wasn't buying my 'this is Juliette' act."

Despite the circumstances, Juliette laughed. "He's known us too long."

"Well, don't worry. I wasn't talking or giving away secrets. He tried a few more times and gave up. It's the giving up part I don't like or trust."

Juliette played with the covers, pushing the comforter into a large hump and smashing it down again. Making mountains out of molehills, she thought wryly. "How about Dad? How're he and Mom doing?"

"Fine. And don't worry on that front either. Dad's not giving away your whereabouts. Much as he respects Stuart, at least for now, he loves you more."

Juliette swallowed over the lump in her throat. "He'll be so disillusioned when he learns the truth."

"Better disillusioned with the snake than confused and worried about you."

Juliette groaned. She knew her parents were concerned she'd called off the wedding without notice or prior suspicious behavior on her part. She'd given no one a clue things were about to unravel with Stuart, mostly because she hadn't had any warning herself. And her sudden vacation wasn't Juliette-like either. She wondered what her entire family would think if they knew she'd taken up with a stranger? A man she wanted to know intimately.

"Have you come up with any ideas on how to reveal this mess with minimal fallout or are you too involved with your fantasy man? My guess and hope is number two—it's why I sent you down there."

Despite her preoccupation with Doug, Juliette had thought plenty about the problems back home. She just hadn't come up with a solution yet. "Actually I met someone who may be able to offer some advice. An impartial third party."

Gillian laughed. "An impartial he or an impartial she?"

"As if you don't know. After all, you set up my fantasy."

"The fantasy, not the man," Gillian said. "So what's he like?"

"Incredibly special." And Juliette had her sister to thank. "What is it you wrote?" Juliette lunged for the night table drawer and retrieved her copy of Merrilee's paperwork, delivered to the cottage upon request. Juliette had been curious what her sister thought she needed in a fantasy.

"Aha. Here it is." She read aloud. "To experience the luxury of being catered to and doted upon by a very special man. To feel desirable, be the center of his universe and forget the hurt of a broken engagement." Her voice trailed off. "How did you know?"

"Because you're part of me. When you hurt, I hurt. And if I'd been through what you just suffered, that fantasy is what I would need."

As twins, they weren't as different as Doug thought, Juliette realized. Which brought another realization to mind. "This trip you sent me on? It's because you feel guilty, isn't it? Because I got involved with Stuart, not you."

She heard her sister's deep sigh. "If I weren't the wilder teenager, the one constantly grounded and in trouble, you wouldn't have gone overboard to compensate. To make sure the reporters had someone else to focus on the times they were out for blood. You took one look at Dad's face when you saw Stuart was interested in you and you saw a way to please him, and you reacted without even asking your heart if it wanted to follow. I feel responsible for that."

"I make my own decisions, even if they're sometimes the wrong ones. You never had to feel guilty." Anymore than she had to overcompensate for her sister's personality. "Oh, the tangled web of our lives." Juliette laughed. "But things always work out for the best. I met Doug."

"Whoever he is, you sound happy. That's all I wanted."

Juliette hugged her knees to her chest. "It's a vacation," she told her sister. "It's temporary." If she said it out loud, she hoped she'd prevent any foolish notions of seeing Doug beyond this week from taking hold. "He's from Michigan."

"Worry about the logistics later and just enjoy for now."

"Oh, I intend to."

"I take it this Doug is the disinterested third party you think can help you formulate a plan to help Dad. You trust him?"

Juliette didn't hesitate. "Yes. I know my history doesn't back me up, but this man's different. And he doesn't know me or my background. He can't possibly want anything except...well, me." She laughed.

"You don't need to convince me. The happiness in your voice speaks for itself. You have fun and don't do anything I wouldn't do."

Juliette rolled her eyes. "That leaves a lot of leeway."

"Exactly," Gillian said, sounding all too pleased with herself.

Juliette hung up the phone filled with restless energy. After washing up, she pulled her hair into a loose ponytail, slipped on the most relaxed outfit she could find, a light-green tank dress and sandals, and headed out the door. Maybe a tour of the island and its lush beauty would ease her spirit. Besides, she needed to kill an hour before any of the resort restaurants opened for breakfast.

The hot, humid outdoors was quiet except for the wildlife, the chirping of birds and slight rustle of trees, making her feel as though she had the island to herself. Half an hour later, her mind was clear, her body relaxed. And then a noisy stirring sounded in the bushes behind her, too heavy and loud to be a lizard or other small animal. Startled, Juliette turned fast, but she didn't see anything or anyone behind her.

"That's strange." She rolled her shoulders, easing the sudden tension. Although she knew the island was private and safe, suddenly she no longer wanted to be so isolated and began a quick walk toward the main building. The entire way the uncomfortable feeling she was no longer alone remained with her.

But when she came upon the pool, her fear dissipated. Doug was alone in the huge pool swimming laps. Pleasure at seeing him replaced every other emotion and she chose a chair at the far end where she could settle in and watch.

He swam with grace and ease, but not with the lazy stroke of a man doing routine morning laps. Instead he hit the water with hard, determined movements, barely coming up for air at one end before diving back under and starting again. Almost as if he were working off frustration rather than swimming for pleasure or exercise.

She curled her legs beneath her and narrowed her gaze, wondering if she were imagining things. But when he finally lifted his head long enough to notice her, instead of a wave, a nod or other greeting, he jerked his head back around and began the harsh routine once more.

7

JULIETTE WAS the last person Doug needed or wanted to see. He turned and hit the water again, determined to work himself until he no longer responded to her fresh beauty or honest eyes. Until his body was too tired to react to hers and his mind could focus on pushing her for answers. Something he'd yet to try.

So far, each time she peeled off a layer of Juliette Stanton, giving him deeper access to her thoughts, feelings and past, he'd let her set the pace. Never pushing. Never prodding. Never probing further than the limits she set, not even when she'd called her ex-fiancé by name. Some reporter, he thought with disgust, and turned at the edge of the pool, beginning yet another lap.

He thought of this morning's call to the hospital and his mother's groggy reply. After the last test on his dad, they'd found clogged arteries that needed bypassing or else he might not survive another attack. They'd performed emergency surgery last night. Unable to reach Doug in his room and he suspected unwilling to try too hard and interrupt his so-called assignment, his mother had endured the hours of his father's surgery and the long wait alone. He should have been there.

And maybe he would have been if he'd been doing his job as a reporter and not falling harder for Juliette Stanton—the woman who held the answers that would free him up from this assignment and let him go home where he was needed.

He surfaced, coming up for much-needed air, to find her kneeling at the edge of the pool. "Exercise doesn't accomplish much if you pass out."

He slicked his wet hair off his face. "I needed to burn off some energy."

"Looked more like you were working yourself to death. What's wrong?" She settled herself on the concrete edge, oblivious to getting her dress wet, and propped her chin in her hands, waiting for an answer.

"Bad news at home."

"Your parents?"

He let out a groan. He had no reason to lie. "My father. He had a heart attack a little while back and they had to operate last night."

"Oh, Doug. I'm sorry." She placed her warm, dry hand over his wet one. "Is there anything I can do?"

He doubted she'd appreciate hearing that information was the one thing he needed. He shook his head. "But thanks for asking."

"Do you need to leave?" The concern in her voice was mixed with a disappointment he couldn't mistake and the anger and frustration he'd mentally aimed her way all morning evaporated.

"Not right now." The surgery had gone well and again his father was resting comfortably. In fact, the procedure might well have added years to his life. "Things are actually looking up."

"I'm glad. I know how much you love them." Relief etched her features. "Of course I'd miss you if you had to go."

With her honest, heartfelt admission, the vise clamping his heart all morning eased as well. He couldn't blame her for the predicament he was in anymore than he wanted to. He'd just needed an immediate outlet for his frustration and guilt. Swimming had helped.

Having her here by his side helped more. "So tell me. What are you doing up so early?"

She shrugged. "I couldn't sleep." She met his gaze and heat flared in her green eyes.

Heat he couldn't misinterpret because the inferno had been burning inside him all night, too. Ever since he'd left her alone in her bed. Walking out when she'd have willingly given herself to him had been the most difficult move of his life. But in the light of day, he could say he respected his actions and, more importantly, respected himself. Given all that had passed recently, that was saying a lot and he had Juliette to thank.

"I had a pretty restless night myself," he admitted.

She nodded without speaking. What was there to

say when silence was comfortable and they could read each other's thoughts? He shook his head, unable to comprehend the bond and sense of understanding she gave him with her mere presence.

He'd always believed his parents shared a unique relationship, one where wedding vows not only meant something but were strengthened with each passing year. In contrast, Doug's few long-term affairs had involved lots of good sex and then demands from the women for him to talk and express his feelings when he'd rather be left alone. He'd always ended up feeling suffocated, needing to get out.

What he experienced with Juliette was special. They shared comfortable silence when he wouldn't mind opening up. She gave him tacit understanding with no strings and no expectations yet he wished she'd demand some. And, most surprising, not only wasn't he sexually involved, but he'd backed off when she'd offered him more. Because he cared more about her feelings and well-being than his own.

"Restless because of your dad?" she asked, seriously, as if she had no clue what walking out on her had cost him.

He shook his head. "I got that call this morning." He'd tossed and turned earlier, thinking of her.

"And now? You're worried and preoccupied?"

"I'm worried, yes. Preoccupied? Not enough to distract me." Not anymore. "I missed you last night."

The genuine pleasure in her smile almost made up for his restless night.

"Well, those old clichés are worth something and absence definitely made my heart grow fonder," she said.

He groaned. "You're killing me."

"I should hope not. There're too many other things I want to do with you first."

Doug knew better than to ask. He knew her answer could only get a man who'd promised himself hands-off in deep trouble. "What things?" he asked anyway, in a voice rough with wanting. Asked as he extended his hand to touch her even though he'd sworn not to.

"Well, for one thing, I want more of those soul-deep kisses you're so good at." Her lashes fluttered as she spoke, modesty rearing its endearing head.

That did it. He grasped her waist and pulled her into the pool. She yelped in surprise and toppled into his waiting arms.

"No fair," she said, sputtering, but she wasn't angry. She was smiling. Laughing, too. His arms remained around her waist as her feet found the bottom of the pool. She pushed down on her dress hem which insisted on floating up around her at the surface.

He chuckled. "Maybe not, but I've finally got you where I want you. You're in my arms and I've cooled you off. Which of those things is a problem for you?"

She splashed a handful of water at him. "Neither, and you know it. It's just your methods that are a little unorthodox."

He splayed his hands in front of him as if fending

her off and grinned. "You said yourself you wanted to experience everything. I'm just helping you along. Besides..." his voice dropped in direct proportion to his deepening feelings, "I want to be with you, too, and right now we're all alone here."

She looped her arms around his neck and leaned against him, bringing them together in a teasing, tempting way. His body, never relaxed when she was around, grew hard with wanting. He'd started this by dunking her, now he could live with the consequences.

"How can a girl argue with a man who'll go to such extremes to get her in his arms?" she asked.

"She can't." He extended his hand, easing her back so he got a full-bodied view. Her light-green cotton dress clung in all the right places and had turned sheer enough to reveal her puckered nipples through the wet fabric. Suddenly those soul-deep kisses she mentioned held tremendous appeal.

"Is this what you meant?" He grasped her face in his hands and feathered a light kiss across her damp lips.

She purred in response. Juliette arched her back until she felt his rigid arousal against her thigh, but his lips lingered and teased not letting her any closer. Nowhere near the heavenly kisses she knew he could give. "Not even close," she murmured.

His laugh rumbled deep in his chest and settled heavily inside hers. "How about this?"

His tongue traced the seam of her lips with languorous strokes. A delicious fluttering arose in her stomach, accompanied by a wave of longing so strong her knees nearly buckled. As his hands threaded through her hair and tugged at her scalp, an erotic rush of sensation and emotion washed over her, then eased away. Much like the water surrounding her now, the carnal stirring beckoned to pull her deeper, yet it remained steadfastly out of her reach. A prelude to the indulgences they could share if only he weren't torturing her with slow and seductive moves.

Since meeting Doug, the wanting and yearning inside her had built to epidemic proportions. Not only did she want to experience the full range of desire, she yearned to do it with Doug—the man who'd given her back both her confidence and belief in herself and relationships.

If she had to stoop low to get him to cave, she had no problem doing so. After all, they'd both benefit.

"Well?" His lips vibrated against hers.

No man could resist a challenge, especially one to his sexual prowess. She felt herself smile as she spoke. "You can do better."

"You have no idea." He grasped her around the waist and hauled her close.

He held her head steady with his hands. His tongue slipped inside her mouth and the explosive fireworks in her body began as he devoured her with a completely masterful, seductive kiss. The kind she'd sought and needed. The kind that left no doubt as to how he felt, no doubt they both desired the same thing.

He splashed his hands into the water, shifting and moving her wet dress until he held her waist in his palms, giving him easy access, enabling him to ease his long fingers upward, to tease the underside of her breasts.

An urgent pull began between her legs, a steady pulsing that resulted in damp heat she recognized despite being surrounded by water. "Oh, my."

He groaned in response. "Are you satisfied yet?" he asked, even as he left a damp trail with his mouth, from her lips, across her cheek until he reached her neck and nuzzled insistently.

She'd never be completely sated, not until he was joined deep inside her. "Satisfied with the kiss?" she asked. "Yes. Satisfied, satisfied? No way." Between kisses, she sucked in a ragged breath. "How about you?"

"Satisfied means you've had enough and I'll never have enough of you." As he echoed her earlier thoughts, the rough timbre of his voice touched her soul. His words touched her heart.

In response, she reached for the waistband of his trunks and slid her fingertips deep inside, until she touched the coarse line of hair on his stomach and the smooth, wet tip of his penis.

"Aah, Juliette."

No man had ever said her name with such passion or reverence. And she'd never needed another man as much as she needed this one. She needed him deep inside her, filling her, easing the ache and emptiness. She pressed her palm down more firmly, then cupped his rigid shaft in her hand, learning his hardness and length, his velvety softness.

Behind her, she heard a distinct rustling of bushes, a sound that brought her out of the desirous haze that had surrounded them. Her surroundings became clear, from the empty pool to the shifting of leaves, a similar sound to the one she'd heard earlier. She jerked her hand free and stepped back quickly.

Doug ducked under the water, cooling himself off, she assumed, while hiding from view. A couple passed the outskirts of the pool, hands held tightly, and neither looked Juliette and Doug's way.

He surfaced and she braced her hands on his shoulders. "That was close," she said.

"We were closer."

She inclined her head. "And does that bother you?"

He ran a frustrated hand through his wet hair but didn't answer.

"Us being intimate and your fantasy... Do they have to be mutually exclusive?" she asked.

He looked into her eyes, his deep blue gaze unwavering. "I'm not sure."

"But I am. You said you needed to see you could put a woman's needs before your own. You've done that with me. Physically, you walked away when your body would rather have stayed. Emotionally too. You've listened to my stories and half answers about my ex-fiancé and my family without ever pushing for more."

He let out a harsh laugh. "It's not like I've bared all to you either."

She smiled and touched his cheek with her hand. "I've told you about my fear of storms and a tree house my dad built. You've admitted you were adopted and explained how you were starving on the streets," she said in a low, soft voice. "That's hardly comparable."

"Maybe not. But you listened to everything I said and you understood without passing judgment." A hesitant yet charming grin edged the corners of his mouth.

"That was easy. I'm interested in you." Juliette made her way to the edge of the pool, her wet dress heavy and restricting.

"Where are you going?"

After pulling herself out, she wrung out the soaked cotton material. She shivered, surprised the air that had been so hot and sticky earlier, could now cause a chill. Especially when her body was still so overheated and warm. "Back to my room to take a long, hot shower."

"Sounds good." His eyes dilated and she knew he had the same longings she did, both of them sharing a steamy enclosed shower together.

And she wanted it to happen. Desperately. But she also knew about waiting for the right time and now wasn't it. He obviously wanted her, but his fantasy was keeping them apart. She looked around for her sandals and saw them floating in the pool. She shrugged, knowing they were a lost cause anyway. "Right now you need space. Time to think. But when I catch up with you later, you should know one thing."

"And what would that be?"

She met his gaze, hoping her heart and her desire were there for him to see. "Our fantasies *can* coexist and I know just how to convince you. By the time I'm finished, you'll no longer be uncertain." She heard the certainty in her tone and realized her bravery and boldness came much easier now. Outwardly, anyway. "And Doug?"

He swallowed hard, his throat moving upward with the force of the movement. "Yes?"

"You won't be unsatisfied either." Before she could blush or tremble or exhibit anything else that would betray her nervousness, she turned and left him alone in the pool.

Alone, unsatisfied and wanting her. But if she had her way, they wouldn't be apart for much longer.

DOUG WATCHED her sassy retreat. He wondered if she realized her outward bravado hadn't fooled him a bit. She was learning boldness as she went along. The closer they became, the more sure of herself she grew. He was glad to know he had a hand in something good in her life.

He took her sandals in one hand and lifted them out of the water. Her laughter when he'd pulled her in still rung bright and cheerful in his ear. She'd been a good sport and they'd had fun. He'd laughed at first, and was aroused the entire time.

Doug hefted himself out of the pool and made his way back to his room. He spent the day reading the paper on the terrace and generally making himself scarce while he digested his situation. His life. His feelings.

Feelings for Juliette. There was no denying her impact. Like a comet, she'd hurtled into his life and, if he never saw her again, he'd never forget the view or its effect on him. Without a doubt, she redeemed him, something he hadn't realized he'd needed. But he'd been a one-track, career-minded nearly lost soul before meeting her. He hadn't thought of anyone's feelings when it came to a story. Except his father's, Doug thought wryly. And the irony wasn't lost on him. Ted Houston had a bigger heart than anyone Doug had ever met. It had taken Juliette to make Doug realize he wanted to be like his old man in more ways than being a journalist.

Juliette. She'd enabled him to forget all the trouble in his life, even if just for brief moments in time. She'd allowed him to feel more than guilt, pain and concern over his father's health and his own personal agenda. More than mere arousal, although the stimulation was carnal and strong and wouldn't abate anytime soon.

And she'd obviously made it her mission to seduce him. She believed if they slept together, he wouldn't be doing so at her expense, but at her pleasure.

His heartbeat tripled and his pulse kicked into high gear. She was as persuasive as she was beautiful. In the pool, he hadn't been able to keep his hands off her, despite his self-imposed promise. And for the first time since laying eyes on Juliette Stanton, he didn't care one bit. Why? He slammed his hand against the bed in his room. Why? Could it be because he was falling in love with his Runaway Bride?

Doug jerked back, reeling as if he'd been hit over the head with a sledgehammer, though a sledgehammer would probably be more subtle. His past relationships had fallen so far short of love, he figured he wouldn't know the emotion if it bit him. But here he was contemplating the possibility. A complication he'd never anticipated, but should have.

He couldn't pin down the moment she'd become a part of his life. He'd been subconsciously studying her each time he'd seen a picture of Juliette and Stuart Barnes, or Juliette and her father, the senator. He'd admired her even then.

He'd been blindsided in Secret Fantasy's lobby a few short days ago. And he'd been putting her feelings, emotions and needs before his own from the minute they'd been introduced. He rubbed a hand over his eyes. So was he falling in love? He had no idea, but he couldn't deny his feelings were strong.

And he hadn't a clue how to handle the emotions

or what they meant for his personal or professional future.

A knock sounded at his terrace door. As if he'd summoned her, he turned to see Juliette. She stood by the closed screen, appearing fresh in her lemon-yellow, loose flowing skirt, camisole and blouse. She was obviously nervous, twisting her hands together, then clenching and unclenching her fists. She couldn't hide her emotions and he loved... Doug coughed. He loved that about her.

He waved her inside. She walked in and slid the screen door shut behind her. "Hi."

"Hi, yourself." He rose from the bed, wondering if her timing had been heaven-sent. To force him to face his feelings before he could go into denial.

"Doug? What's wrong? You're looking at me like you've never seen me before."

An apt description. She could read his thoughts too well. He needed to push those emotions to the back of his mind and concentrate on what Doug, the reporter, needed.

As if. There was no way he could maintain that promise to keep his distance any longer—because that promise had been made a lifetime ago. Before his earth-shattering revelation. And with each passing second, his certainty grew. He'd fallen in love with Juliette Stanton.

Had he been blindsided? Definitely, but he could list the reasons he'd fallen with ease. She was every-thing he'd never experienced in a woman and everything he desired. Fresh, unjaded, despite past hurt, and as open and honest as she could be under the circumstances. She knew how to reach out to him when he was in pain and just being around her eased his distress.

He remembered the time his father had attempted to encapsulate his relationship with Doug's mother. Always a man good with language, sensible words had failed him. "Your mother has the screws that fit the holes in my head," Ted Houston had said. Doug had merely stared at his father, baffled by the description he'd thought was crazy when he heard it. One he'd never truly understood, not even after going through several unsuccessful affairs of his own.

More snippets of that father-son conversation came back to him now. "She listens to me, son, and that's rare in a woman, believe me. So if you find one that listens and understands, that's more than half the battle." Ted had laughed. "The other half doesn't need mentioning. Your hormones'll make their opinions known but your head and your heart will lead you in the right direction."

His father was right. Doug's hormones didn't need mentioning. But he'd been following his heart from the minute he'd laid eyes on Juliette in the lobby, letting her set the pace, allowing her to ask the thought-provoking questions, putting her needs before his own. His head had taken over last night, forcing him out of her cottage and away from her bed before he did something they both might regret later.

He thought of his father's words and how they related to Juliette. As he'd told her this morning, she'd listened to everything he said. Without passing judgment, she'd been there and she'd cared. He exhaled a slow groan. The tables had turned. Though he still needed information, still wanted to be able to look himself in the mirror, he already *knew* with certainty he could and would put Juliette first.

Because he loved her.

He extended his hand and led her inside. "Welcome. It's not as big as the cottages, but it'll do."

She glanced around, taking in the dark wood furniture, hardwood floors, beige decor and smiled. "It's so masculine. So you. Makes you wonder if Merrilee matches people with rooms as well as with their fantasies."

He laughed, though he felt anything but light with his secrets, lies and omissions standing between himself and what he was coming to realize was his true fantasy—Juliette herself.

He didn't ask himself where that put his story and professional future. He already knew he had no answers. "So what brings you to my end of the world?" he asked her instead.

She caught her lower lip between her teeth. "I need to talk to you."

"Sounds ominous."

"It isn't really, but you need to bear with me." She paced the room and he remained silent, giving her the time she seemed to need. Finally, she settled herself on his bed, knees curled beneath her. "I'd planned to do this the seductive way, but I'm finding I can't."

Her simple button-down shirt was opened to reveal a mere hint of lace, and yet it was supremely seductive to him. This woman could be covered from head to toe and he'd still get hot and bothered just looking at her. But she obviously had more on her mind than tempting him right now. "What is it?"

"What's more intimate than sex?" she asked.

Hearing her say the word, he nearly choked right there. "I'm not sure. You tell me."

"Truths. Secrets. Private revelations. Once two people reveal those, they've shared something deeper and more meaningful than a physical joining. You've already given me that intimate gift by sharing your past."

He nodded, unable to speak. He'd told her a lot, but he hadn't revealed all. Doug inhaled deep. "Go on."

"I intend to reciprocate." Her wide eyes bore into his. "And once I do, we'll be on more even footing. I'll have let you inside me, so to speak." An incredible flush stained her cheeks a bright shade of red. "And you'll know for certain you've put me first."

How could he believe he'd completely put her first considering the lies and omissions that stood between them? That and his guilt. Neither of which he'd figured a way out of yet. And neither of which she knew anything about.

So, he resisted the urge to touch her. If he didn't exercise restraint now, he'd take her right now on this bed and satisfy both of their fantasies at their personal expense. He needed to hear what she had to say first. Needed this intimate, emotional bonding she wanted to give him. And not for his story or career. What he'd do with those truths, he'd have to deal with later.

She inclined her head and a red curl eased over one shoulder, as she inched closer on the bed until she sat next to him, until her heady scent surrounded him and set his already raw nerves on fire. "And once you believe you've gotten your fantasy, then we can make love."

"Juliette." What he meant as a warning came out resembling a low growl.

She merely smiled. That sexy, I-know-it-all smile. Only she didn't.

Sleeping with Juliette would be the answer to a dream, his and obviously hers, too. She wet her lips with her tongue and he followed the movement, recalling doing the same thing this morning, tasting her in excruciatingly slow detail.

And that's how he'd make love to her, Doug decided. Excruciatingly slow, exquisitely tender. He wanted nothing more. But he curled his hands into tight fists, knowing he'd never be that free. Not until he'd admitted all. And he hadn't figured out how to do that without losing her forever.

"I've got secrets that no one knows. Not another

living, breathing soul except my sister, because there's been no one I trust. Until now. I trust you. Because you've put me first. You've made me feel cherished and special."

"That's because you are." Doug swallowed a curse. He was in purgatory, that awful place between heaven and hell.

"Thanks to you, I believe that. But in case you're wondering why this sudden revelation, it's not just about getting closer to you. I need your advice. Because what I'm about to tell you can affect so many people's lives."

He cleared his throat. "I have to admit you've piqued my curiosity." Little did she realize the people whose lives would be most affected by her revelation sat together in this very room.

Doug the reporter was on the verge of gaining the information he needed—the very reason he'd traveled to Secret Fantasy to begin with. Doug the man was on the verge of being in Juliette's arms and inside her body.

Yet all of him was teetering on the brink of losing everything he now realized he held dear because he was gaining that information in a deceitful way. Something he'd known going into this charade.

But it was no longer a charade, no longer a means to salvaging his career. It was his life. She was his life and he didn't want to lose her.

8

"MY NAME is Juliette *Stanton*." She said the name as if it ought to mean something to him.

Tread the fine line of truth, Doug thought. "Senator Stanton's daughter."

She inclined her head. "He's quite a public figure, isn't he?"

Doug heard the love and caring in her voice. "He's one of the few politicians who can claim a good political and moral record. I can see a lot of you in him," he said softly.

"That's a nice compliment." She smiled. "You haven't made the connection yet. Could it be the news hasn't reached Michigan?"

Another lie coming back to bite him. "You're Chicago's infamous Runaway Bride. I made the connection, I just didn't want to make you uncomfortable."

"You didn't recognize me then?" He couldn't mistake the hope in her tone.

He grasped on to his first day on Secret Fantasy and fingered one spiral curl with his finger. "The hair's different than the pictures."

She glanced down. "Everyone thinks I bolted because I got cold feet. Or I had a lover on the side. Did you know local radio stations in Chicago are holding contests? It was ridiculous. I couldn't leave my house without being followed. Don't people have anything better to do than focus on my life? I'm not even a celebrity." She shook her head in disgust.

"You never know what's going to strike people's interest."

She lifted her head and met his gaze. "You haven't asked me why I ran."

"If you want me to know, you'll tell me." When she looked back on this conversation he wanted her to be able to remember she'd revealed without being pushed or prodded. That he hadn't forced or directed the conversation in any way.

Because when she found out the truth, not only didn't he want her hurt, but he wanted her to be able to forgive him.

"I do want to tell you. I just don't know where to begin."

Her pain was palpable and Doug had no desire to prolong the revelation any longer than necessary. "I know about the newspaper articles fingering your ex's business partner in a money-laundering scheme."

She winced. "Then you know the article was retracted due to lack of proof."

He merely nodded.

"I believed Stuart was innocent. I believed his partner, Congressman Haywood, was innocent."

"So the retraction must have been a blessing."

"At the time it only confirmed what I already knew. But later..."

Doug held his breath. Here it was, the answer to his story. The one that would put him back on top, ease his father's emotional unrest and fix the damage he'd done to the *Tribune*'s reputation. That damned guilt warred with anticipation deep inside him.

Juliette stared off into the distance. "We'd gotten to the church early to do that last-minute family thing. But I was getting claustrophobic and I left my mother and sister in the back chamber because I needed air. The church wasn't filled yet but I didn't want to run into anyone, so I went out the back to a place Stuart, Gillian and I used to hang out when we were kids. That's where I saw them."

Adrenalin rushed through his veins. "Saw who?"

"Stuart, Congressman Haywood and Paul Costa." She clenched and unclenched her fists. "The article in the paper alluded to Mob connections and money laundering but it didn't mention anyone by name. But Costa is an alleged boss and there's no way I wouldn't recognize him. And then there was the snippet of conversation I overheard. Something about the retraction being taken care of and the reporter silenced." She shivered. "There was no question what Stuart was involved in."

Doug listened to her in disbelief. His gut had told him she knew something to link Barnes and Haywood to illegal dealings. He'd never once thought she'd been an actual eyewitness.

"Did they see you?" At the thought, his stomach began to churn.

"Would you miss a bride in her fluffy white wedding dress?" she asked, her voice dripping with sarcasm. "Actually Stuart caught sight of me and excused himself. I'd already ducked back inside and he grabbed my arm and led me to someplace private. We had a huge argument. I called off the wedding and he…" She inhaled deep.

"He what?" Doug grasped her hands, warming them inside his. He had his story. Now he needed to take care of Juliette. And later he'd figure out how to tell her the truth without ripping her heart and trust to shreds. "Did he threaten you?"

She shook her head. "I don't think I'd be as torn or confused about what to do if I'd been his target. He said if he went down, he'd make sure he took my father with him. An implicit threat to keep my mouth shut."

And knowing Juliette's strong feelings for her parent, something Stuart Barnes had to have known, he'd easily guaranteed her silence.

Doug squeezed her hands tighter. "Forgive me for asking this, but is your father involved in anyway?"

"No. But if Senator Stanton's handpicked protégé is arrested, it'll taint my father's record and any good he's accomplished in his term. *He* might be innocent, but he'll go down in history as leaving office surrounded by scandal and suspicion."

Doug let out a slow groan. Her admission had just

called a glaring halt to his plan to expose Barnes and his Congressman partner at all costs. A blunt article with Juliette as his witness would destroy her father. And anything that hurt Senator Stanton would kill Juliette. Something Doug would never do. The tough-guy reporter he'd been before meeting this woman was long gone. Doug had to accept that truth—one a long time in coming. As long as he'd been on this island.

Damned if he had a plan right now, but he had to come up with one and soon. Although he had all his personal excuses for wanting to nail Barnes and Haywood, a more pressing reason remained—he couldn't let their illegal activities go unchecked. And he had to expose them before Barnes was elected senator. A good possibility considering his being jilted at the altar would garner him the sympathy vote and, as of now, Senator Stanton was still in his corner. He had to halt the senator-elect, without hurting either Juliette or her family.

"You're quiet. I've shocked you."

He shook his head. "I always knew you were special. But the lengths you went to to protect your father, the flak you took from the media..."

"He'd do it for me in a heartbeat. That's why I need to figure a way out. I can't let Stuart become senator, knowing what I do. And I can't hurt my father. I need your help and input. Together we could come up with an idea." She hesitated. "But I was also hoping we could do something else together first." Her voice had dropped a husky octave and the atmosphere shifted.

The room temperature inched up a heated notch and sexual vibrations surrounded them. Doug went from concerned to aroused in seconds flat. Apparently Juliette felt the same because she inched up onto her knees and moved near, bracing her hands on his shoulders and placing her lips close to his ear.

"Can you see the enormity of this secret? That I wouldn't share it with just anybody?"

If she only knew who she'd just trusted. The guilt was enormous, though he tried to console himself with the fact that he was on her side. "Juliette..."

"Doug..." She parroted in a low murmur. "You've made me feel like I can trust you with anything. That has to mean something in the scheme of your fantasy."

It meant she believed she could trust him and though *he* knew that was true, he was still deceiving her, something she'd never understand. "Fantasies are complicated," he said.

"They don't have to be." She nuzzled the sensitive place behind his ear with her lips and he let out a slow groan.

Irony was at work again. She'd revealed all in order to bring them closer and though he needed time and space to sort out what he'd learned and figure out the best and safest way to use the information, if he walked out on her, he'd hurt her as badly as his secrets would. Secrets he couldn't reveal until he'd figured out a way to help her, save her father's reputation and secure them as a couple.

"Doug, if your fantasy is really about putting a woman's needs first...make love to me."

All the restraint he'd exercised vanished in that instant. She'd freed him mentally and emotionally and he refused to look back. He would figure a way out—after he did as she asked and made love to her.

Grasping her hips, he took control, toppling her onto her back on the bed. "You've been testing and teasing me for two days now." Now it was his turn.

Excitement danced in her eyes. "Oh yeah? I know I've tried. I was thinking I didn't have much success."

"Sure you did." He swung his legs over her waist, pinning her to the mattress. "It's just that I've got what's called discipline."

A smile worked at her lips. "Looks to me like it's gone."

She had no idea.

Her pelvis rose, her feminine mound pressed intimately against his hard erection and she let out an appreciative moan. "It feels that way too," she practically purred.

Maybe she had a better idea than he'd originally thought. "You're wearing too many clothes," he muttered. Silk skirt and top, both soft and feminine, but a barrier just the same.

"Then take them off me."

A provocative suggestion if he'd ever heard one. She spread her arms out at her sides, treating him to an even more provocative pose. Her button-down blouse revealed a lace garment beneath. Soft webbing that reminded him of sexy lingerie and hot nights in bed.

And this night was about to get much hotter.

Juliette stared into Doug's deep blue eyes, unable to believe how close they now were. How intimate they were about to become. She'd confided her most private secrets and she had no doubt he'd help her figure out her next step. Just as she'd obviously helped him figure out his.

Fantasy accomplished, she thought with pride— both his and hers. Yet she was still here—breathless, nearly panting with her heart galloping fast in her chest and her mind playing out erotic fantasies at Doug's hands. And those hands now dipped enticingly beneath her blouse, pausing when he encountered the lace camisole. Tingling awareness shot through her as he chartered covered territory.

With nimble fingers he explored until he found her breast, full and aching for his touch. "No bra?" he asked.

"Not necessary with so many layers." Her lack of undergarments had been a conscious, planned decision, because when she'd decided to trust him with her secrets, she wanted to trust him with her body as well. In a way she'd entrusted herself to no man before. She was exposed to him in every way that counted.

He glanced down and nodded in approval. "Easier access for me."

Her body heated with his innuendo. "That was the plan," she said, feeling a burning blush rise to her face.

Doug took her off guard by pressing a gentle kiss to her heat-flooded cheeks. Then he leaned back, aligning their bodies as close as possible, despite the barrier of clothes. Heavy and full, his erection teased her empty body with tempting possibilities.

"How would you like it, Juliette? Slow or fast?" His voice came out a low growl that both excited and aroused.

And here she'd thought she was already on the edge and at her most sensitive. "I think we've already taken things slow enough, don't you?"

In response, he grabbed the ends of her shirt and yanked hard. Buttons scattered and material ripped beneath his strong hands and the sound tore through her much the way desire clawed inside her.

He grinned. "I aim to please. After all, I'm here to make your wishes come true."

She licked at her dry lips. "Did you know there's a saying? That every woman has a caveman fantasy buried deep inside."

"Then, by all means, let's fulfill yours." He spread her shirt wide, revealing her breasts to his gaze and the cool air.

She'd looked in the mirror earlier, seen her nipples,

dark and erect beneath the lace material. From the tight pull of his jaw, he saw too—and he liked it.

"What would your caveman do after he dragged you back to his lair?"

"He'd kiss me." Desire, stronger than she'd ever known, pulsed in rapid cadence, begging for release. Liquid moisture wouldn't be denied and trickled between her legs.

"Kiss you where?" Doug asked. "He can't satisfy you if he doesn't know what you like." He watched her intently. And he waited. All the while he drew slow circles around one darkened nipple. Teasing. Arousing. Waiting.

Her body bucked and she trembled. Juliette swallowed hard. "I thought we agreed on fast."

"You tell me what you'd like and I promise you fast and hard and deep."

At his words a soft cry escaped her lips and his blue eyes darkened to a stormy hue. "Where would he kiss you?" he asked again.

Could she really admit her deepest longings aloud? She questioned, yet she'd already trusted him with far more. How could she deny him or herself now? "He'd kiss my breasts," she murmured.

True to his word, Doug pressed a light kiss against one distended peak, followed by wide laps of his tongue, and after he'd thoroughly laved her nipple, he began a harder, flickering motion. One that caused a quickening in her stomach and an intense, direct pull between her legs and had her squirming beneath him.

He gave her "fast." He gave her "hard."

Juliette knew "deep" would come.

She hadn't realized she'd shut her eyes until she felt her camisole being pulled up, and when she raised her back off the mattress, he slid it over her head. Goose bumps prickled at her bare skin.

"You are so beautiful." His husky voice nestled deep in her chest, perilously close to her heart.

Embarrassed, she averted her gaze. He took her chin in his hand and turned her to face him. "I am not your ex. I don't want you for your father's senate seat or any other reason. I want *you*."

She didn't question the link he'd made. She'd given him enough information to connect the dots and draw the not-so-pretty picture. But his words made up for all the pain and ugliness in her past.

"When I look at you I see the woman I...admire." He splayed his hands over both breasts, pressing her nipples into his palms and cupping her completely. "The woman I care about."

The woman he loved? The word popped into Juliette's mind without warning. Without thought. But then when did an onslaught of emotion pause to announce its presence? She had the unsettling hunch it was her own feelings she was thinking about though. If she was really thinking at all. She couldn't tell, not when her body seemed to all but take over her mind.

And her body demanded so much more. She

reached for the waistband of her silk skirt. Taking the hint, Doug rose off her, long enough to shuck his jeans as she did the same with her elastic-waist skirt.

He turned back to face her and sucked in a startled breath. "No panties."

"Easier access, like I said." She shrugged, trying desperately not to appear as self-conscious as she was feeling. She bit down on her lower lip. "I notice you're not wearing underwear either."

In fact he was gloriously naked and completely male. Juliette discovered he was all hard muscle and erect steel. She tried to swallow but found the lump in her throat was too great.

"Difference is, I *was* wearing some." A wry smile twisted his lips as he stepped toward the bed.

Her heartbeat tripled. "But you aren't now."

She blinked and found herself covered by his naked body, his warm skin and his even hotter, rigid flesh. Her body molded to accept his harder shape and contours and she absorbed his raw, masculine scent. He bracketed her head in his hands and his lips met hers in a dizzying kiss. He held nothing back as his tongue delved into the recesses of her mouth. Her body recognized the prelude of what was to come, filling with need, bursting with desire.

He eased his hands between her legs and his fingers did a slippery glide into her feminine heat. His earthy groan reverberated through her. "I promised you hard, fast and deep," he murmured.

She raised her hips, letting him know she was ready.

His sexy smile was devastating. "And I always keep my word." After reaching for protection, he reared back. His eyes darkened as he spread her thighs wide and entered her with one demanding thrust.

Juliette shut her eyes and intense sensations took over. She felt him—thick and hard inside her, pausing to let her adjust and shifting so she could take him farther into her. Her heart seemed connected to her body as fantasy and reality meshed and melded into one.

She nearly peaked then and if the guttural sound that ripped from his throat was any indication, he was close too. But her emotional reaction was far more potent than the physical sensations rocking her body. Because joining with Doug rocked her world.

She wasn't a virgin but she might as well have been, so new and enlightening were the feelings and emotions clogging her throat.

Love.

There was that word again. But she had no time to process the meaning. He raised himself up, slowly, allowing her to feel the exquisite sensation of his enlarged member gliding out of her, and giving her body time to moisten and stretch farther to accommodate his size, length and intentions.

Instinctively she bent her legs to keep him inside her. Keep him a part of her. "Doug." She whispered his name as he drove himself home—hard, fast and deep, just as he'd promised.

"Is this what you had in mind?" He slid out again only to return with more force than before.

"Yes." She'd been waiting so long for this moment, for this man, that climax wasn't far off. The waves crested, higher and faster, washing over her entire being until she was beyond thought, beyond reason.

He found the perfect rhythm, but this time he raised himself above her, bracketing her head and holding his weight with his hands, so all she felt was *him*, moving inside her, hard and hot, thick and firm...

Her hips jerked up to meet each incredible thrust. She forced her heavy eyelids open. The emotion she saw in his eyes and the taut expression on his face matched the emotions rioting through her.

"Doug, please." She wasn't even sure what more she could want.

"Deeper?" he asked, his deep voice barely controlled.

"Oh, yes."

"Then help me out, sweetheart."

She wrapped her legs around his waist, pushing her femininity into him, so each consecutive lunge buried him more fully within her. "Faster." She spoke the last on a gasp for air.

He complied, moving faster and harder, taking her up, up, up and over, into a burst of blinding light and waves of unending ecstasy. He let out a loud groan, her climax triggering his. Or maybe he'd been waiting for her, but they came in unison, his hot breath on her cheek and her name on his lips.

Minutes later, cocooned in Doug's arms, her heartbeat slowly returned to normal. But Juliette knew without a doubt that everything else had changed.

After Stuart's betrayal, love had been the last thing she'd believed she'd wanted or thought she'd ever find. Her fantasy—once she realized she had one— was to get past the hurt and know she was desirable, not because of her family or political connections, but for just being her. But she *had* fallen in love instead. Fallen fast, deep and hard.

And now that she had, she refused to take a wait-and see attitude with her life and her future. Perhaps her newfound determination to take charge had something to do with Stuart's demand that she keep silent, and his absolute belief that she would comply. Or perhaps it had more to do with loving a special man who she refused to lose after this vacation was over. At least not for lack of trying.

So although she'd keep silent about Stuart, at least for now, she had every intention of telling Doug she loved him. With a little luck he felt the same and happily ever after wouldn't be a farfetched notion for Juliette Stanton, Senator Stanton's daughter.

DOUG LAY AWAKE long after Juliette had dozed off. He inhaled, taking in the fragrant scent of her hair and the musky reminder of all they'd shared. They'd skipped dinner out and called in for room service, then made love one more time. Although his body was temporarily sated, his heart wasn't even close. How could it be when too much was uncertain?

He needed to know they had a future and the only way that could happen would be for him to come clean and hope she could find a way to understand and forgive. Considering she'd been hurt recently by a man who'd used her, Doug had his doubts. But he refused to lump himself in the same category as Stuart Barnes because Doug loved Juliette and had never set out to hurt her. He stifled a wry laugh. He was a master at using people for professional ends and if he lost his greatest desire now, it was probably no more than he deserved. Because, initially, he *had* set out to use her—no matter what his reasons or how good his intentions seemed at the time—just like her ex-fiancé.

She sighed, stirring in his arms. He brushed her tangled hair off her face and let her curl more snugly against him. He might not know what she ate for breakfast when she was late for work or how easily her living habits would gel with his, but he had no doubt they could make a long-term commitment work. And he was certain he wanted not just to have an affair or to live together but a till-death-do-us-part commitment like his parents shared.

His certainty was born of his past. He'd never experienced anything as all-encompassing or strong as what he felt for Juliette. And he couldn't mistake the difference in his feelings for his past lovers and his current love.

Careful not to wake her, he eased himself out of bed. She shifted and resettled, snuggling against the pillow. And he pulled a resort pad out of the desk and began jotting down notes. Ways to protect Juliette, the eyewitness, from harm and ideas for his current story.

He wrapped things up, tucked his notes into his suitcase and crawled back into bed. To his delight, Juliette immediately rolled back into his arms. Minutes later, her breathing evened out. Slow and easy, he knew she was asleep.

"I love you," he whispered, knowing he had the freedom and wanting to test the words out loud for the first time. They felt right and certainty filled him once more. He shut his eyes and let himself relax, his body slowly matching her rhythm.

Morning would come soon enough and with the break of dawn, his truths. And Juliette's reaction.

But he woke up alone with a note propped against the clock, covering the digital numbers. At least she'd attempted to make sure he wouldn't miss her message. He stretched, reaching for the white paper.

It's my understanding most men don't like a woman to spend the night.

Wanted to avoid an awkward morning after, so I went back to my room to shower and change.

Breakfast at my place? Door's open.
Juliette.

                    P.S. Last night was incredible.

Incredible didn't begin to describe it. Doug crumpled the paper in his hand.

He wasn't most men. Not when it came to one specific woman, anyway. He'd not only wanted to wake up next to Juliette, he'd wanted to be the one to do the waking. In a sexy, sensual, arousing way meant to show her exactly how he felt—before he lay his truths and life in her hands.

But breakfast had its advantages, too and, being a writer, Doug was an inventive man. He could come up with all sorts of erotic ways to enjoy a meal that would leave Juliette with no doubt about his feelings. After a quick shower, he headed out the terrace door and around the back, to the path leading to a congregation of secluded cottages.

Doug had been a reporter for longer than he could remember. Ever since meeting Ted Houston, digging for a story had become a part of him. Watching people. Listening carefully for hidden meaning and innuendo. He knew how to follow at a discreet distance and because there were often other reporters on the same trail, Doug knew when he had company.

And that same uneasy feeling pricked at him now. Here on Merrilee's secluded island, Doug wasn't alone and he wasn't talking about other guests of the resort. They wouldn't be in hiding. He glanced around but already knew he'd see nothing out of the ordinary. He also knew the rustle of bushes he'd just heard wasn't a bird or animal.

Instead of going directly to Juliette's, Doug decided to test his theory. He circled back toward the pool, choosing a rarely used path that was overgrown with vines and greenery. Not a trail someone following him could take without being heard and, sure enough, when he'd made it halfway, the rustling noise began, then stopped suddenly, repeated itself and then silence descended. Whoever was behind him had begun to follow and stopped when the person realized Doug was on to him. A rank amateur to be sure.

Doug darted back to see if he could catch the interloper, but whoever it was had obviously anticipated Doug's move and was nowhere to be found, giving him cause to rethink the amateur label. Whoever had followed him might have made more noise than a bull in a china shop, but had been quick enough to avoid capture. Silence now surrounded him, unbroken but for the chirping of birds and an occasional laugh from someone walking by.

But Doug never discounted gut instinct and if he needed proof, hadn't Merrilee said she'd fit some people in at the end of the week who'd seemed more desperate than most? He hadn't a clue who'd come down here, but he knew one thing for sure. All candidates led to Juliette. And none would appreciate finding her with the reporter who'd broken the original story and who had the potential to destroy them now. He needed to narrow down the list and fast.

Another journalist was his first thought. Not likely. If the person had managed to get the story, he was talented enough to remain out of sight and hearing. And besides he'd be watching Juliette more than Doug.

It could be Congressman Haywood if Stuart had blabbed to his business partner about what Juliette had seen and heard in the church. Not a likely candidate either. He'd send Barnes, Juliette's ex, to exert influence if she was wavering.

Which led him to Stuart Barnes checking up on his errant ex-fiancée. More likely. And as a squeaky clean senator-to-be, one dumb enough to get involved with the Mob, he wouldn't be smart enough to let other people do his dirty work. And once he put the pieces together he'd be more interested in Juliette than Doug.

The Mob. Damn. Doug hadn't any idea if they knew about Juliette or not but he wasn't taking chances and took off at a run. He had to get to Juliette and make sure she was safe. Then he had to reveal his own truths—not just because he loved her but because she needed the knowledge to protect herself from all converging outside forces.

Including Doug. But with the word *Mob* echoing in his brain, at this moment he'd settle for just seeing she was safe.

9

JULIETTE LET the room service waiter out of the room and set the table on the terrace for two. He'd delivered the setting and promised he'd return with her breakfast order, fresh *mimosas* included, as soon as she called. As soon as Doug arrived.

She inhaled deeply. Orange bird-of-paradise surrounded the patio and she'd accented the table with fresh hibiscus. Their fragrant, aromatic scent lingered in the air. She was filled with more hope and optimism than ever before and she had Doug to thank. In her sleep last night, she dreamed she'd heard him say those three magic words.

And if she was lucky she'd hear the phrase again, but this time she'd be awake and Doug would be looking into her eyes and meaning every word.

In the meantime, her feelings floated out there, changing her perspective. Juliette saw things more clearly now—she had from the minute she'd told her story to Doug. Clarity came from talking out loud to a neutral third party, far away from Chicago and her problems. And she'd realized she didn't need to hide the story, she needed to inform her father. The man had an uncanny knack of understanding and sorting out problems. He'd be disappointed in Stuart and his choices, but he would never put a criminal in the Senate.

She shook her head, amazed she hadn't seen the solution sooner. Confide in the man who'd instilled her with values and let things sort themselves out from there. She wondered if she was deluding herself about the simplicity of it all. Wondered if love was just making her view of the world rosy, or if she'd truly found some sort of realistic resolution.

Another thing to discuss with Doug, along with her newfound feelings. She smoothed out a wrinkle in the tablecloth, excitement building at the thought of seeing him again. But she had no desire to have him find her still rumpled and messed from last night's activities.

Heading inside, she selected her outfit for the day and, after laying it out on the bed, stripped off her clothes and stepped into the steam-filled bathroom, then shower. Hot droplets pelted her skin and she reluctantly let the water rinse away any remnants of last night's lovemaking. But knowing last night was just the beginning allowed the tingling anticipation to build all over again.

"Juliette."

She thought she heard her name being called and grabbed for the shower curtain to cover herself.

"Juliette." The voice sounded again, only this time she recognized it as Doug's.

"In here." Knowing he was her visitor relaxed her.

Until the bathroom door slammed open and she realized she'd given him permission to join her. In the shower.

"You're okay?" he called into the bathroom.

"Why wouldn't I be?" She slipped open the curtain, poking her head out but still keeping herself behind the opaque barrier.

He leaned against the doorframe, disheveled and out of breath. "You're alone." His relief was tangible.

She shook her head, damp strands touching her shoulders. "Who would be with me? What's wrong with you?"

"You shouldn't leave your door open," he muttered, moving closer.

She inhaled the potent scent of sweat and man. "Been running a marathon?" she asked jokingly.

He kicked off his shoes and stripped off his shirt. Ripping the shower curtain open wide, he stepped inside, heedless of the running water, unconcerned about his remaining clothes.

His strong arms wrapped around her, pulling her close. "I thought...never mind what I thought," he said as he covered her mouth with his.

Juliette sighed and molded into him, letting him take control. He devoured her with his kiss and his hands roamed her body as if he didn't quite believe she was okay. She didn't know the reasons behind his obvious fear and concern but she had to admit she liked his possessiveness when directed her way. "I'm okay."

He stepped back. "We need to talk."

He had to be joking. He'd invaded her shower, treated her to one of his mind-blowing kisses, aroused her body and now he wanted to talk? She reached for the snap on his shorts. "Talking's overrated."

"Juliette."

"Did I ever tell you what that low growl does to me?" She popped the snap and undid his zipper, pushed his shorts and briefs down. "It's a sexy sound."

One he made again as she wrapped her palm around his already hard erection. "There are things you need to be aware of," he said.

"Later." She pressed a kiss against his bare chest. "The hot water only lasts so long and I want to take advantage."

More like she wanted to take advantage of him, Doug thought, helpless against her tender yet arousing touch. He kicked off the clothes encircling his ankles. Though he did need to level with her, now that they were alone and he knew she was safe, the news could wait a bit longer. Her lips traveled a steady line downward from the center of his chest past his abdomen and lingered so she could tease and torment him with her tongue.

He leaned his head back and groaned. As long as they were together, she would be safe, he told himself, and waiting another hour to tell her the truth wouldn't matter. Then nothing mattered at all. She gripped his waist with her hands and she circled his erection with her mouth, using her lips and tongue with full, loving strokes to bring him to the brink of insanity.

He'd never expected such an incredible gift and knew he sure as hell didn't deserve her openness and giving. He also refused to go all the way alone. As incredible as she made him feel now, he'd much rather be inside her body.

He lifted her to her feet and then into his arms, taking them out of the slippery tub before letting her slide down his body to stand on the floor, slowly, so he could revel in the feel of her softer body against his. Her full breasts pushed against his chest, her nipples puckered and peaked.

"What was that about?" she asked.

Eyes glazed, voice husky, she aroused him more. Even the chill didn't bother him in the least, not when he was so hot for the woman in his arms.

"Leverage." He backed her to the wall, bracketing her shoulders with his palms. "No way can I do what I want with you in the shower."

A slow, sexy smile worked its way onto her lips. "Do tell."

"I'd rather show you." Bending his head, he kissed her sensually and completely, all the while moving his hips in maddeningly slow circles against her waist. His body strained for completion as he thrust against her over and over again.

She let out a moan, then caught on quick, matching

his movements and countering them at the same time. She pressed and pumped her feminine mound against his erection, creating such intense friction with their lower bodies he thought he'd come right then. Her ragged breathing and carnal sounds matched the demanding tide rising inside him.

He paused only to open the medicine cabinet and take care of protection. He'd already discovered even this amenity had been supplied by the resort. Then unable to wait, he grasped her hips, lifting her up, and with deft jockeying of position, he lowered her onto him at last.

She cocooned him in damp, moist heat, sheathed him in slickened tightness. "Sweet heaven."

She trembled and wrapped her arms around his neck and her legs around his waist. The wall behind her gave him the additional leverage he needed to keep the rocking, gliding motion going. His body, buried deep inside hers, felt full, thick and ready to burst and when her first tremors of climax began, she clenched him tighter in her velvet heat.

The erotic contracting of her muscles brought him up and over the edge, triggering an explosive orgasm. One that engaged not only his body but his mind, his heart and his soul.

JULIETTE LAY in bed with Doug drawing lazy circles with her fingers across his chest. Silence echoed around them but she didn't feel the need to talk. What they'd just shared spoke for them. Contentedness reigned and she had no desire to change a thing until the ringing of the telephone jarred her, bringing her out of her blissful state.

She grabbed the receiver. "Hello?" she said, and discovered the hotel kitchen was calling to double-check her order and ask when she'd like it delivered. She sighed, knowing reality had just intruded and the time had come to gather her courage and face Doug with her feelings. "Five minutes would be perfect," she told the man on the other end of the phone.

She hung up and turned back to Doug. "Breakfast," she explained. "I invited you, remember?"

He rolled over, covering her with his warm weight. "I thought we just ate." As if to back up his words, he began a steady nibbling on her lips that he knew she couldn't resist.

"Mmm..." She sighed into him, kissing him back, not ready or willing to break their physical connection just yet. But with room service on the way, she had no choice. With a gentle push, she encouraged him to let her out from beneath him. "I'm sure you can work up that appetite again."

"I most definitely can." His hand reached down and cupped her breast.

A languorous wave of pleasure rushed over her. "Room service is coming," she reminded him, but not easily. "I wanted to surprise you, though that's impossible now. But give me a few minutes to finish setting up, okay?"

In reality she needed a few minutes alone to gather

her thoughts—because over breakfast, she wanted to admit her feelings and see where things stood between them when this week was over. She couldn't do that if they were lying in a bed that carried the musky scent of their lovemaking or if she let the heat of physical release sway his emotions. She needed both of them thinking clearly.

"No problem." But his reluctant groan contrasted with his words. "I need to check in at home first anyway." His deep blue eyes bore into hers. "But we do need to talk over breakfast."

Something in his voice caused a shiver to take hold and she wrapped her arms tighter around her. "Sounds ominous. But yes, we do need to talk."

She pulled herself out of bed and wrapped the satin robe around her naked body before starting for the bedroom door.

"Juliette."

She turned. "Yes?"

"It's only ominous if you take it that way."

She inclined her head and let herself out, his cryptic statement ringing in her ears.

Juliette stepped through the living area to the terrace to discover the waiter setting down her order. As if by magic, he'd appeared within minutes of his phone call. She shook her head, amazed by Merrilee and her staff's efficiency. After placing the order on the table, the waiter left, leaving Juliette in peace.

She poured the drinks and unwrapped the basket of rolls, croissants and Danish, recalling the last time she and Doug had discussed the merits of *sweets*. Then, they'd exchanged an erotic prelude of things to come. A prelude to this morning, when she'd tasted him more thoroughly than she'd ever imagined, given to him in a way she'd never felt inclined to give to another man. Including her ex-fiancé.

"Hello, Juliette."

"Stuart!" She thought she'd conjured his voice, but she turned to find herself facing him. Shock and disbelief rippled through her. "What are you doing here?"

"Fulfilling a fantasy, same as you." He stepped onto the patio, his shiny loafers gleaming in the sun. He wasn't dressed down as most of the guests; rather, he wore a pleated pair of tan slacks, a designer belt and his usual well-pressed collared shirt.

His staid, conservative dress only made her glaringly aware of her own lack of clothing and she pulled the collar of her robe tight around her throat. "What kind of fantasy would bring you down here?" she asked, certain his visit had nothing to do with fantasy and everything to do with her.

"You remaining silent, of course." His piercing stare bore into hers. "Not that I told Ms. Schaefer-Weston that."

Juliette wasn't surprised Stuart had fed Merrilee a story. He had probably used an assumed name, too. Merrilee's ethics were too strong for Stuart to gain access to Secret Fantasy any other way. Glancing at him now, Juliette recalled her sister's words about how his sudden silence had unnerved her and Juliette inhaled deep. Now she was the one shook up—by his unexpected presence and the lengths to which he'd obviously gone to join her on the island resort.

She swallowed hard. "I already said I wouldn't expose you. Any reason you couldn't take me at my word?"

"Your sudden disappearance concerned me. It's not like you to run."

His dual implication wasn't lost on her. "It wasn't like you gave me a choice. You lied to me and a marriage has to be based on trust." And on love, Juliette thought.

She supposed in a way she ought to be grateful for the revelation at the church. If not for her last-minute discovery before she said *I do*, she would have realized eventually that what she felt for her own husband was not real love. Because now she knew what honest and true love felt like. It was what she felt for Doug.

"So without the marriage vows, how do I know I can trust *you?*" he asked wryly.

"Because you know me. You have known me for years." She didn't miss the irony. She'd known him for an equally long time yet she'd been blindsided by his lies and illegal associations. Would Stuart realize the incongruity as well? At the very least she prayed that he wouldn't suspect she was misleading him, that she'd already revealed the details of Stuart's shady dealings to Doug, and that she planned to tell her father as soon as she returned. The senator, Juliette assumed, would take the story to either the police or the press. Either way, Stuart wouldn't be seeing the election ballot, never mind her father's Senate seat.

But she had known him for years. Which led her to a lingering question. "Why, Stuart? Why get involved in dirty deals and money laundering?"

He shook his head. "You really don't get it, do you? Maybe we grew up next door to each other but you grew up with the money and the spotlight. I had to *work* for it."

"And you did. You worked hard and you made it. You're almost there."

He sighed. "I figured Bob's connections would give me the money to back me up as well. But what they say is true. Before you know it, you're in too deep."

"So get out. It isn't too late."

"It is unless I want to lose everything. I won't let that happen. And your silence will make sure my dreams come true." Stuart picked up a leafy hibiscus she'd laid on the table, twirling it in the air, examining the petals. "So what's your fantasy? What are you looking for that I didn't give you? That I knew nothing about?"

She forced a laugh. They'd known so little about each other it was pathetic, Juliette thought. In less than a week, Doug understood her better than Stuart had after a lifetime.

She shrugged. "Gillian surprised me with the trip. She created a fantasy. I'm just living it out," she said, hoping he'd leave it at that.

"It involves a man."

Juliette raised her eyebrows, wondering how he'd known, then silently berated herself. Between her skimpy robe and the intimate setting she'd staged, she'd given herself away. "I can't imagine you're jealous. Not when all you saw in me was a stepping stone to easier election."

Since he'd reluctantly admitted as much at the church when he realized there would be no ceremony, Juliette saw no reason to couch her words now.

He shook his head. "Jealous is the wrong word." He reached out for her hand, but she stepped back, away from his touch. "I'm serious, Juliette. I *am* concerned. You need to watch the company you keep and what you say. Otherwise no matter how much *I* may believe you'll keep quiet, I won't be able to protect you."

"I have kept quiet, and your concern is touching but unwarranted." She leaned on the white chair, gripping the cool wrought iron for support. She wasn't comfortable lying anymore than she was complacent with his trip down here and his so-called concern. "I'm not involved with anyone that's a threat to you or your partners." She said the last word with disdain.

"If that's true, then how about sharing the name of the man you're...involved with?" Stuart said.

She stopped herself from glancing back toward the inside of the house and giving Doug's presence away. He could walk out at any moment or she could yell and he'd be by her side in an instant. But she refused to make a scene when she could possibly avoid one.

She didn't believe Stuart wanted to hurt her. He just needed to pacify his well-founded fears. "Whoever I see is no longer your concern."

"I told you I'm worried about you."

Juliette laughed. "More like you're worried about what I might reveal."

"That goes without saying, considering who you're involved with." He stepped closer, watching her closely.

"First you ask me who I'm involved with and now you sound as if you know. Well, which is it?" she asked, running out of patience for Stuart and his games.

"I asked if *you* cared to share the name. I wondered if you even knew."

"Of course I know. It's Doug..." she said, her voice trailing off. "I don't know his last name." She admitted that truth reluctantly, hating to give Stuart any more power over her.

"Houston," Stuart said. "Douglas Houston, the *Chicago Tribune* reporter that broke the initial story."

Impossible, she thought, shaking her head. Her stomach cramped but she ignored the pain. "You're confusing him with someone else. His name is Doug, yes. But he's from Michigan, not Chicago."

Yet he hadn't revealed his last name, Juliette thought. Not even after she'd bared her soul and admitted her deepest secrets. Not even after they'd made love had he shared something as basic as his last name. Her heart shouted it was a coincidence but her head reminded her she'd been hurt and used before—by the man standing in front of her.

"He's a reporter," Stuart said firmly. "And if he's been spending time with you down here under false pretenses, he's a liar as well."

"You're one to talk," she muttered. "Doug's a...writer," she said, her stomach plummeting once more. He'd followed in his adopted father's footsteps, he'd said. "And his family?" Juliette asked in a soft voice. "Are they reporters, too?"

"Journalists through and through. Are you satisfied now?"

She believed him but she was by no means satisfied. Betrayal twisted her insides and self-disgust took hold. When would she learn? She was not a good judge of character when it came to men. She never had been, never would be.

Juliette lowered herself into the nearest chair. "Go away, Stuart. You came and made your point. Doug is a *Tribune* reporter and the last person I should reveal my secrets to. And now that I know he's as much a lying snake as you are, you have nothing to worry about, right?"

Pure relief washed over his face. If the situation didn't make her feel so pathetic on her part, she'd have laughed out loud.

He stepped toward her and knelt down. "You have to know I never meant to hurt you. We were friends and I thought we could have a good life."

She shook her head. "I have nothing more to say. That ought to make you ecstatic, right?" She waved a hand, dismissing him.

"You're smart, Juliette. You always were. And you love your father. In this case, that combination will serve you well." His implicit threat made, and apparently having gotten what he came for, Stuart was happy to be gone, leaving Juliette alone with the painful truth.

She'd fallen in love with another man who'd used her for his own selfish ends. Ever since his original article was printed, then retracted, Douglas Houston's name wasn't worth squat. Another lovely word courtesy of her sister's students. But one that fit. And Juliette had just foolishly given Doug back his entry into Chicago's political circles.

She'd given him the information he needed to back up his original story and clear his muddied name. Information that would crucify Stuart and his partners, and set herself up as a walking target should any of them discover that, not only could she connect them, but she'd blabbed their secrets as well.

DOUG WATCHED Barnes's retreat. His heart in his throat, he decided to give Juliette a few minutes to digest the information and pull herself together before facing him. It was the least he could do.

Hell, he needed to do the same. He'd been too damn complacent, Doug thought. Too sated by their incredible lovemaking and then caught up in his mother's concerns over his father's health.

He'd been distracted, which had dulled his reporter's instincts, and he'd never expected to come upon Stuart Barnes and Juliette. Having locked the doors when he ran inside earlier, he'd never thought she'd head out to the patio alone. He hadn't been thinking, period.

And when the sound of conversation drifted toward him from outside, Doug prayed he'd find the waiter serving breakfast. He wasn't so lucky. He'd stepped closer to discover Stuart Barnes had paid Juliette a visit.

Though Doug hated ceding control, he'd quickly realized he had no choice. Should he make himself known, he'd risk Barnes jumping to the correct conclusion—that Juliette had already spilled her news. So he opted to wait and take his case to Juliette later when they were alone. Opted to allow her to make clearheaded decisions without his presence distracting her. So he'd remained out of sight, knowing he could protect her if the need arose. But nothing could alleviate the feeling of helplessness he'd suffered as truths that should have come from him were revealed in a way that gave Doug no chance for damage control. He'd listened as his future had been slowly but surely destroyed.

He had to admit Juliette had given her faith in him her best shot. His gut had clenched as she'd attempted to deny Barnes's claims—an admirable defense of a not-so-admirable man, Doug thought in disgust.

He'd wanted to put her first. He'd wanted to be able to look himself in the mirror. He shook his head. He'd never be able to face himself again.

Hell, facing Juliette now would be the beginning of his life-long punishment—a life that didn't include her. He stepped out of the shadows and into the direct sunlight on the terrace. "Juliette."

She swung toward him, her normally bright eyes dull, her expression blank. "It seems we haven't been formally introduced," she said, rising from her seat. "We both already know who I am." She extended her hand but remained stiff and formal.

His stomach twisted, but not knowing what else to do, he placed his palm inside hers.

Like she was facing a stranger, she pumped his hand firmly in a cold grip, then released him. "I'd say it was nice to meet you, Mr. Houston, but that would be a lie." Hurt, betrayal and disbelief were all evident in her gaze.

But one thing was more painful than the rest. After all they'd shared and as intimate as they'd been, not only did Juliette look at him as if she'd never seen him before, but she looked as if she couldn't stand the sight of him.

"I'd like to explain."

She glanced away. "The obvious needs no explanation. At least that's what my dad always says. Then he lets us explain anyway, so you might as well go ahead." She waved a hand dismissively, as if he were a child wanting to justify bad behavior.

Which, he supposed, he was. He reached for her hand and she stepped back from his grasp. Frustrated, he shook his head. "Why do I get the feeling nothing I say will make a damn bit of difference?"

"Should it?" Juliette paced the ground of the small patio. "Why don't I make it easy for you? You had a story to tell and your name to clear. I had the information. Simple."

"If you think back I never once pumped you for that information."

She rolled her eyes. "As if you had to. I made it so easy."

"It's called sharing, Juliette. You said it yourself. We shared the most important things in our lives— my childhood and your recent past. I'm a reporter but I never asked you one leading question. Don't you want to know why?"

She studied him but he couldn't read anything in her closed expression. His heart pounded furiously in his chest as he grasped onto his last chance. "I love you."

A flash of emotion lit her eyes along with a sheen of

tears. "Fool me once, shame on you; fool me twice, shame on me." She drew an unsteady breath. "But I do have to admit one thing."

Ridiculous hope flared in his chest. "What's that?"

"Not only does your reputation precede you, but you should be proud. You're damn good at your job."

Doug clenched his jaw, pain radiating straight to his head. He'd bared his soul and she didn't believe him. Not that he blamed her. She was right. He'd done his job too damn well.

"Juliette..."

"Whatever it is, it doesn't matter." She swung around, placing her back toward him.

He could have dealt with anger, disapproval or outright accusation but he got none of those. Instead he received apathy—the one thing he couldn't fight. The one thing that would keep him at arm's length now and maybe for good.

"Can you just leave?" She wrapped her arms around herself, protecting herself from him.

No matter how much *he* knew he was the last person who would hurt her, *she'd* never believe him. At least not now.

"I want you to understand something first. I came for a story about your ex. I never intended to hurt you. Never planned to use you..." he said, his voice trailing off, knowing how lame his words sounded.

And knowing despite his best intentions, using her was exactly what he'd done, exactly what he'd planned, no matter how he'd excused it at the time.

And if he'd thought beyond his own needs he'd have realized hurting her was inevitable. "I'll go."

If she deserved nothing else from him, she deserved to have her wishes granted. She deserved to have him gone.

JULIETTE TOSSED the last item of clothing into her suitcase, then zipped it closed. *Let loose and be yourself,* she thought with disgust. She'd come to a conclusion that had nothing to do with self-pity, just fact—apparently it didn't matter if she played the dutiful daughter, the politician's fiancé or Juliette Stanton the woman, all were ripe for being used.

When a knock sounded at her door, Juliette exhaled a sigh of relief. She'd booked an evening flight back to Chicago today and had called for someone to bring her luggage to the main part of the hotel. But instead of a bellman, she found Merrilee on the other side of the door.

"I understand you're checking out early," the older woman said. Questions and compassion mixed in her gaze.

"My plans changed." Juliette stepped back and let her visitor inside.

"Life rarely goes according to plan."

She shook her head and laughed. "You can say that again." She hadn't expected to fall hard for any man, especially another one who'd lied to her from the outset.

"Would you believe me if I told you that the unexpected often works out better than anything you'd planned?"

"At this moment? Probably not." Juliette forced a laugh and started to cry instead. The emotion she'd held in check for the last couple of hours came rushing out, sweeping over her in full force.

Merrilee put a hand on her back and Juliette attempted to wipe away her concerns as easily as she could swipe a hand over her eyes and dry her tears. But neither could be dismissed so easily and she found herself reliving her fantasy by confiding everything about the past few days to Merrilee.

"I feel ridiculous." Juliette said when she was done, sniffing and grabbing for a tissue.

"I don't know why. We've all been through bad times. But why are you so sure Doug didn't mean what he said? 'I love you' isn't something a man says easily."

"It is in my experience," she muttered.

"Your ex-fiancé?" Merrilee asked.

Juliette nodded. "Stuart's 'I love you' was a way to make himself a part of my family and keep himself in my father's good graces."

"And Doug's? I admit I only know what I see, but he genuinely seems to care about you."

"He also wanted something from me."

"Which he got. And has yet to use," Merrilee reminded her.

"Yet being the operative word."

Merrilee patted her hand. "There're many ways to tell a story. Do you want my advice?"

Juliette nodded. With her sister and parents too far away to help, Juliette would take whatever advice this kindhearted woman wanted to give.

"Keep an open mind and, most importantly, an open heart," she said, her eyes fathomless, seemingly wiser than her years. "Are you sure I can't persuade you to stay longer?"

Juliette let out a sigh. "No. As beautiful as this place is, I really do need to get home. I've been sitting on some things too long and need to take action." She debated telling Merrilee about Stuart and decided against it. Fate worked a certain way for a reason. At least now Juliette was in possession of all the facts.

"Well, I hope in time you'll look back on your stay here fondly," her hostess said.

"Believe it or not, I already do." At the very least, she'd learned plenty about herself and her ability to open up and trust, even if it had been with the wrong man.

But if he was so wrong for her, then why did the pained look in his eyes linger in her memory along with his words? *I never intended to hurt you. I never intended to use you.*

I love you—the last said long after his lies had been exposed. She hugged her arms around her waist. Long after he'd walked out, leaving her alone as she'd requested, she'd replayed every moment of their time on the island in her head. Every touch, every kiss, every intimate conversation.

No question he'd come to Secret Fantasy with an agenda, but could his feelings have shifted midcourse? Hers most certainly had. "Merrilee?"

Her hand on the door, the other woman turned. "Yes?"

"Do you have any regrets in life?"

She nodded. "Not having had the chance to follow my heart."

Her words rung in Juliette's ears long after Merrilee let herself out. *I love you.* Lord knew, his lies aside, Juliette loved him. But she'd been taken in twice. Both so recent she still had the scars to show for her misplaced faith. How could she even think about trusting the words and expressions of a man whose lips and eyes had already deceived her?

10

IF FLYING from Secret Fantasy to Miami, from Miami to Chicago, and Chicago to Washington D.C., all in forty-eight hours, was enough to prove love, Doug would have Juliette in his arms by now. Unfortunately, Juliette had gotten a head start and the last seat on the last flight out of Miami. After hours of waiting in airports and too little sleep, Doug prepared himself to face Senator Stanton's secretary and then the senator himself.

In fact, his journey had just begun. And when he stood in front of Juliette's father, he understood just how difficult the trip would be.

Senator Stanton rose from behind his desk. "I shouldn't even be seeing you." Despite the older man's graying hair and age, Doug saw similarities to Juliette. Like his daughter, even in disapproval, his green eyes held an inherent warmth.

Doug extended his hand and the Senator shook it warily. "I take it you've spoken to your daughter," Doug said.

"Long enough to know you've been busy."

He accepted the intended criticism with a nod of his head. "Not as busy as I might have been if I'd spent the last day and a half writing an article instead of traveling to find you."

"Then I'm sure you have something important to say." Senator Stanton gestured for Doug to take a seat, then settled into the leather oversize armchair behind the desk. "Don't tell me you traveled all this way to warn me about your exposé. Journalists don't usually extend such courtesy."

"Especially ones who've hurt an innocent woman, you mean?"

"Touché. And your words, not mine, but in this case they'll do fine."

"Sir, I have an idea that will keep your daughter out of the paper completely. My paper, at least. I can't control what others print but I can damn well control what *I* write." And thanks to Juliette and her warmth and sensitivity, she'd taught him to give his words careful consideration.

The older man leaned forward in his seat. "And why would you want to do that?"

Doug drew a deep breath. "Because I love her," Doug said the words out loud for the second time in as many days.

His heart pounded hard and fast in his chest as he realized just how much he cared for the redheaded beauty. Just knowing her had redeemed him. Having her love would make him whole. The man sitting across from him was his only chance at proving his worth and his word to the woman he loved. He cared more that Juliette believe she hadn't let herself be duped again than he did about the lonely life ahead of him if she turned him away. Something he had no desire to face. He stood before her father, hoping the older man's reputation for fairness and understanding would hold long enough for Doug to make his point. After that, all bets were off.

Senator Stanton tapped his pen against his cedar desk. "Assuming I believe you—and, to be honest, I'm reserving judgment—don't expect me to go to bat for you. Juliette deserves to make up her own mind—especially regarding the issue that you hurt her badly, yet proclaim to love her."

Doug nodded. "I wouldn't have it any other way. Besides, I'm a writer. I expect my words to speak for me." Or rather, the words he left out of his article would speak for him, Doug thought. Because, if things went as planned, he could print his exposé and never once mention Juliette Stanton's name.

"You'll have to use more than fancy words to sway my daughter now."

Doug glanced at the older man. He'd dealt with the senator before but never on such an intimate level and he both respected and liked the older man's defense of his child.

"May I add one more thing, sir?"

The senator nodded.

"I wouldn't presume to ask you for a thing, except your approval if I can get your daughter to come around to my way of thinking on her own."

Reluctant admiration lit the older man's gaze. "I've

only just come into possession of the disturbing truth about my protégé. Then I heard about your more recent role." The older man met and held Doug's stare—an imposing man who held an imposing position in the country, but it was his role as father that was the most intimidating now. "You know, under other circumstances, I might like you, Houston."

An unexpected grin worked at the corners of Doug's mouth and he laughed, feeling more optimistic than he had since leaving Juliette on Secret Fantasy. "Give me ten minutes and you still might."

"MMM, THIS is delicious. I haven't had a good bagel in..."

"Over a week," Gillian said, laughing. "Didn't you eat on that island?"

Juliette chewed and swallowed the dough and cream cheese. Her father had returned home for the weekend in time for meetings and Sunday breakfast with his girls. Four days had passed since her return with no word from Doug. No news at all, she thought.

Not that the Runaway Bride bit had gotten old. The reporters still staked out her home and followed her around, speculating this time on why she'd disappeared for a few days. They'd traced her as far south as Miami. Apparently Merrilee had managed to fudge things from there. A miracle as far as Juliette was concerned, but it was only a matter of time until all things came to light. But at least here at the family home at eight a.m., things were quiet. A typical family breakfast wasn't news.

But Juliette appreciated her family these days more than ever. "The island was different. We had sweet stuff there, like danishes." And kisses, Juliette thought. Delicious, intense, soul-deep and prolonged kisses.

"And Florida orange juice, I'll bet," Annabelle Stanton said. "I think we're overdue for a vacation, don't you, Len?"

Her father covered his wife's hand. "Next break, okay?"

Juliette watched the easy give and take between her mother and father, the genuine love and caring— and her heart, already bruised, came close to breaking. She'd wanted that, wanted it for herself and Doug. No matter that they'd known one another a short time, she'd believed they each had enough strength to make a relationship work. But she hadn't counted on the lies.

Her mother shook her head. "Don't lie to me, Len."

An eerie feeling swept over Juliette as she listened to her mother's laughing words.

"We'll plan a trip and then something will come up and you'll have to stay close to D.C." Annabelle laughed once more. "Don't think I don't know the routine. Tell me what you think I want to hear and hide the rest so I'm less hurt and disappointed in the end."

They were an old married couple who knew one

another so well, they accepted each other, faults and all. Juliette shivered.

"At least retirement's around the corner," her mother continued. "Girls, do you think we can keep your father so busy he won't miss Washington?"

While Gillian and their mother began a recitation of activities her father enjoyed, he leaned closer to Juliette. "One week at home and I'll be climbing the walls."

She laughed. "You'll survive, Dad. There's plenty of good you can do outside the Senate."

"That's my girl. Always worried about the right thing to do. If I'm not mistaken, that's how you ended up engaged to Stuart." He laughed but his eyes were concerned and serious. "Maybe it's time you take the less politically correct road."

She rolled her eyes. "I told you already. I tried something like that and ended up hurt." Juliette had gone straight from the airport to her father's house because he was leaving for D.C. in the morning and what she had to tell him couldn't wait.

They'd sat up for hours, she, her mother and father, Juliette alternately crying and unburdening herself like she had as a child. He'd been disappointed and disillusioned in Stuart, yet understanding about calling off the wedding. He'd just wished she'd come to him sooner to spare herself the ensuing pain. As for what happened next, her father had promised not to make a move until he gave the situation careful consideration and until he figured out a way to protect everyone who could be damaged by the information. But he was aware of Doug's possession of the news and therefore knew he had time constraints on his actions.

Juliette wondered what had gone on over the weekend but wanted just a normal family breakfast too badly to ask now. Reality would intrude soon enough. She looked around at the people closest to her. She was so lucky, so fortunate with the lot she'd drawn. Unlike Doug. The thought came unbidden.

"Juliette."

She hadn't realized her father was calling her name. She shook her head. "Sorry. I was distracted."

"By that man."

"*That man*, has a name." Juliette glanced up to see her father grinning. "I don't know what's so funny," she muttered.

"He affects you, honey. That's not funny, it's serious."

"Tell me something I don't know."

Everything about Doug affected her—his touch, his warm breath in her ear, and when they lay flesh to flesh, the way his heart pounded against hers, like they were one. And when his body joined with hers, they *had* been one. Juliette trembled. The good memories affected her most and made it difficult to believe everything had been a lie, part of an agenda to get a story.

"Sounds to me like you two have unfinished business," her father said.

She clenched her hands at her sides. "What's unfinished about the pretense under which he went to the island and the lengths he went to get his story?" she asked.

But as she sat with her family, with the people she'd been closest to since birth, she wondered—what other awful things besides hunger had Doug endured on the street? What other events had shaped the determined, driven man he'd become? And she wondered too what role *his* love for his adoptive parents—especially his ailing father—had played in the desperate means he'd used to get Juliette's story.

Her father shrugged. "Only you would know what's unfinished. Or whether what was said between you two is more important than what went unsaid."

I love you, he'd said. And she'd remained silent in return. *We shared the most important things in our lives—my childhood and your recent past.* And she'd made a mockery of his admission.

"What have you learned from your mother and my relationship?" her father asked. "The most important thing we've taught you girls?"

Juliette realized her mother and sister were listening intently but neither were interrupting. Quite a feat for Gillian, but she obviously realized the importance of the conversation and respected it.

"You taught us to follow our hearts," Juliette said softly.

"And did you? With that guy in college? Or, more

importantly, with Stuart? Did you follow your heart? Or what you thought your mother and I wanted you to do?"

A rhetorical question and they both knew it. With Stuart she'd been the dutiful daughter. But with Doug... Merrilee's one regret in life came back to haunt her. Not having had the opportunity to follow her heart.

Juliette began to shake inside, unable to speak. With Doug, she had followed her heart and it had led her to a man she'd believed was outside the problems in her life. A man who'd enabled her to loosen up and be herself. A man who'd helped her overcome her fear of storms, she thought glancing out at the pouring rain and remembering the electricity they'd generated together. And the man she'd let in—not just into her body, but into her heart.

The man she'd let go. Did she honestly want to look back as Merrilee did and realize she'd let the opportunity to follow her heart pass her by? The trembling turned into full-fledged shaking as she wondered if it was too late.

"I want to take a look at this morning's paper," her father said. A lifelong politician, he knew how and when to beat a hasty, strategic retreat. He gestured to the countertop and the newspaper he'd picked up from the driveway earlier.

Juliette needed a minute away from her family's caring but prying eyes. She swallowed over the lump in her throat. "Sit tight, Dad. I'll get it," she said, then padded in her heavy socks over to the stack of papers.

The morning headline shouted out at her, Doug's byline prominent and clear. Retracted Retraction, side by side with Exposed! Congressman's Dirty Dealings Revealed. Her stomach did a flip at the sight of Doug's name and photo. In the body of the article was another picture—one of Stuart and Congressman Haywood, together.

Her reaction to seeing Doug, even in a small black-and-white photo—and more clean-shaven and conservatively dressed than she'd known him to be—told her how greatly he'd affected her life. Her skin blazed hot and fire licked at her soul.

If she thought she'd missed him before, the missing piece of her heart grew wider now. Problem was, she was facing not just Doug's picture, but his article. He'd obviously used the information she'd shared with him. Her stomach plummeted in dismay and disappointment, but her pulse picked up rhythm.

Follow your heart, her parents had always said. And hers was refusing to give up on Doug despite the evidence in her hand.

She glanced over her shoulder, seeking her father's support, but he was engrossed in conversation with her sister. She didn't need his advice anyway. If she really loved Doug, she had to believe in him—in his last words to her on the island and what she'd seen in his face that final day.

She gathered her courage and handed the paper to her father.

"Aren't you going to read it?" he asked.

Juliette shook her head. "I have all the answers I need in here." She tapped lightly on her chest.

Her father rose and gave her a hug. "You made the decision with your heart. Now as your father, I'm here to tell you it's the right one. When you do get around to reading that article, I'm sure you'll fall for him all over again." His voice sounded gruff and parental at the same time.

Juliette hugged him back and ran for the door. "Where are you going?" Gillian called after her.

"For a run in the rain." And an exercise in overcoming her fears.

If Doug was up for another lesson.

Only after Juliette got into the car and pulled onto the road did she realize she had no idea where he lived. Though she knew where the *Tribune* offices were located, there was little chance he'd be in at this hour on a Sunday. With no destination, she headed to the heart of the city and parked about a block from the *Tribune* offices and sat. Talk about impulsive, spur of the moment, ridiculous moves.

With her heart pounding hard in her chest, she reached for her cell phone and dialed information but, of course, Doug's phone number was unlisted. So she did the only thing she could—she called Merrilee, the woman who made fantasies come true.

DOUG HAD BEEN exonerated as planned and his father was home from the hospital, recuperating and in high spirits.

So why did Doug feel so let down? He retrieved the newspaper from the front stoop of his condo and tossed the paper onto the table in the kitchen. The events of the past few days had culminated in the article of his career, thanks in large part to Juliette's father.

Per Doug's suggestion, Senator Stanton had approached Stuart Barnes, his protégé, the man he'd groomed and cared for, and had talked him into turning himself in. He'd convinced Barnes that his self-respect was more important than a Senate seat, and whatever he'd done by joining with Haywood and his associates, could be undone. In return, the senator had promised to remain by Barnes's side throughout—if he came clean now. The younger man had gone to the police and Doug was certain any high-priced attorney could turn Stuart's willingness to give up his partners into a reduced sentence.

Doug wasn't surprised how easily Barnes had been won over by Senator Stanton's charm and sincerity. After all, hadn't Doug been won over by the man's daughter in a matter of hours?

Meanwhile Doug's article had been an exclusive, redeeming him and exposing the Barnes-Haywood Mob-related corruption scheme—all without a mention of Juliette Stanton's name. And without using the

Runaway Bride angle of the story the other papers had been clamoring for.

Of course the answer to why Juliette bolted from the altar could be found by deduction but it wasn't a subject Doug had chosen to bring up. He'd sacrificed that tidbit of news in favor of protecting the woman he loved. Sacrificed. When had Doug Houston ever sacrificed the meaty details to protect someone else? He had to admit, he felt damn good about himself now and could thank Juliette for teaching him to be more caring. And with an exclusive exposé under his belt, under any other circumstances he'd feel sheer satisfaction.

Instead, all he experienced now was a profound sense of loneliness and frustration. For a man who'd always been on his own, who'd never even had a live-in relationship, he should be used to a solitary existence. But choosing to be alone and being forced into the state were two very different things.

Needing a change of scenery, he decided fresh air might clear his head. Doug grabbed for his keys and hit the street only to discover a walk in the rain—even a walk down Lake Shore Drive, far from Secret Fantasy—brought back a flood of memories. All of them good, none of them ever to be repeated again, because fantasies by definition were created by the imagination and not meant to be lived out forever.

And besides, he'd fabricated his fantasy in order to get himself paired with Juliette. He'd told Merrilee that by helping Juliette heal, he'd see he could put another person before himself. He'd said he wanted to make up for using Erin to further his professional aspirations. And he'd claimed he needed to be able to look himself in the mirror. The irony was, as he'd spoken aloud, he'd realized he was telling the older woman the truth.

Yet all he'd done was repeat his past mistakes. He'd used Juliette exactly the same way he'd used Erin, only this time, he'd also been hurt. He'd fallen hard and lost the woman he loved. Well deserved, Doug figured now.

The biggest irony was he'd achieved his fantasy and still wasn't satisfied. The fantasy he'd woven for Merrilee had helped him become more human. Yet even looking back and understanding every place he'd gone wrong still didn't hand him the future he desired. That decision was out of his hands. After all that had passed between them, if Juliette wanted him, she knew where to find him. Or did she? It wasn't like he'd shared that important bit of information. He muttered a curse and headed back toward home, wet for his troubles, but no closer to a solution.

As he neared his front step, he caught sight of fiery hair gleaming in the mist, making him wonder if even undeserving S.O.B.'s like him sometimes got second chances.

He slowed his pace as he approached, still feeling as if he were in a dream. But when she extended her hand and he touched her, he knew she was here. Real.

And, he hoped, his fantasy come to life.

"Hi there," he said.

"Hi, yourself." A hesitant smile pulled at her lips, a smile he'd missed in the past lonely week.

The rain began to pick up momentum and he dug into his pocket for his keys. "You're sitting in the rain. Is your fear of storms wearing off?"

She shrugged. "Better memories have taken over."

Her hand remained in his and he held on tight, brushing his thumb over the pulse point on her wrist. "Have you been waiting for me long?" he asked.

She licked at her damp lips. "Only all my life."

Without another word, he pulled her to her feet and let them inside. He swung her around and, backing her against the wall, they met in a scorching kiss that was emotional and intense and left him without a doubt that her feelings were as strong and potent as his.

"I missed you." Her softly spoken words echoed in his ear as she nuzzled her head between his shoulder and cheek.

"Likewise." He reached for her waist and pulled her body close to his. "I know we have things to work out."

"Mmm." She murmured in agreement. "Lots of things to settle." Her lips created havoc with his nerve endings while she feasted on the sensitive skin of his neck. "But nothing that can't wait."

His body was already anticipating his next move and he desperately needed that emotional and physical connection. Needed to feel himself inside her and know they were real. "Waiting to talk is good." He thrust his body against hers. "Waiting for anything else is not."

"I'm not the one wasting time talking," she purred in his ear.

No, she was the one with her hands halfway down his pants. From modest to confident, all in the course of a...relationship? He'd have laughed at the change if the entire subject weren't so serious.

She wrapped her hand around his erection and he let out a groan. The lady had a point. There was a time for talking and now wasn't it.

He looked into her green eyes, darkened by desire and an emotion he hoped he could name. "Race you to the couch?"

"Well, it's about time." She laughed, ducked beneath his arm and ran for the sofa, losing clothing on the way.

Doug followed her lead and ended up on top of her on the couch, her body heat seeping into him and warmth filling the cold spaces inside him. Spaces that had been cold far longer than since she'd left him on the island. And spaces only she could ignite and rouse into a burning flame.

He raised her arms above her head, linking his fingers with hers. "No protection."

"It's not a problem for me. How about you?"

He heard the challenge in her words. In the past he'd have felt like he was being trapped, that the walls were closing in. Instead, euphoria lifted him higher. "You don't sound too upset about it."

"Should I be?" She shifted, spreading her legs in an invitation he couldn't mistake. "I was half asleep one night on the island. We were together and I could have sworn I dreamed you said something important. And then you said it again, only I was awake but not ready to hear. If you meant it, I need to hear you say it again."

Her voice shook and Doug recognized her fear and anxiety about putting herself out there to be hurt if she was wrong. He understood because he'd been there himself. Only neither of them would ever hurt the other one. Not if he had a say in things, and it seemed now he did.

He eased his hand down, slipping his fingers into her silken, moist heat. She let out a soft sigh of need, but her gaze never left his, her eyes wide and imploring, the question still lingering between them.

"No questions, no uncertainties between us, Juliette. Never again." He raised himself over her and entered her with one smooth stroke. "I love you." As her muscles contracted around him, the words came not from his body but from his heart and they'd remain there. Forever.

Juliette felt herself toppling over the precipice quickly, the incredible waves building with each successive thrust of Doug's body inside hers. And when she fell, she knew he was there with her. But long after the physical satisfaction faded, Doug's words remained lodged in her heart.

He'd grabbed for an Afghan blanket on the arm of

the sofa and covered them and now she lay cuddled in his arms. "You have to know I love you, too."

"I kind of figured that out about the time you lost the last item of clothing on the way to the couch." He laughed, but sobered quickly. "I just don't understand how I could be so damn lucky after what I did. That article must have been much better than I thought."

She needed to look him in the eye so she rolled to her side, a mistake since she nearly fell onto the floor. She settled for climbing back on top of him instead. "I never read the article."

His eyes opened wide and she felt the rapid increase of his heartbeat beneath her chest. "Then what the hell changed your mind about me?"

"You did." She ran a hand down his cheek. "You said you loved me when you had nothing more to gain. It was something I should have realized and believed in long before Stuart ever showed up."

"I used you."

His honesty now touched her. She inclined her head. "You came to Secret Fantasy for a story. You didn't leave the moment you got one. Any other arguments?"

He clenched his unshaven jaw. "My fantasy was a lie—at first."

"And later?"

His hands cupped her cheeks. "I wanted to put you first and I wanted to help you heal. Instead, I repeated old mistakes and hurt you even more." In the depth of his eyes, she saw his pain.

In hurting her, he'd hurt himself. If that wasn't love, then Juliette didn't know what was. "Oh, Doug. Loving me isn't hurting me. Who hasn't made mistakes? I made mine when I followed some nonexistent plan I thought my parents had for my life. The only bright spot is that it led me to you. Oh, and that fantasy of yours? About putting me first and making my dreams come true? Did I mention I'd like you to keep it up for the next fifty or sixty years?"

His hands held onto her hips, preventing her from falling, and his deep chuckle reverberated inside her. "Is that a proposal?"

"Damn straight, since you might have just gotten me pregnant." This time she made sure her challenge was light and fun. She had him and she damn well knew it.

He grinned. "No way can I turn down a proposal like that. Especially from a woman who accepts me the way I am."

"Darn right I do." She turned serious. "How's your father?"

"Home and eager to meet the woman who's turned me inside out, upside down and made me inhuman since she's been out of my life."

Her heart kicked up a beat. "Sounds like someone's missed me."

He let out a heartfelt groan. "You have no idea. But you do realize, you don't even know if I squeeze the toothpaste from the top or the bottom."

She laughed. "Are you trying to scare me off?"

He shook his head. "I'm realizing it'd take a lot

more than my living habits, thank goodness." He brushed a light kiss over her lips.

"We have a lot more to discover about each other." As if to make her point she slipped her hands downward in a slow, leisurely exploration of the body she adored.

"And we've got a lifetime to learn." He greeted her hands-on journey with some incredible moves of his own, causing her to writhe and squirm on top of him.

"Well, I'm game." She managed to speak through the desire quickening inside her.

"And I'm glad." Love shone in his eyes, making her feel complete. "But don't you think you ought to read that article?" he asked. "There's nothing in there about you. Not a word, not a hint, not a mention. Just your father's wisdom."

Her father. He'd said when she got around to reading the article she'd fall for Doug all over again. At the time, she thought he was applauding her courage for going after the man she loved, but she realized now her father probably had a hand in working things out with Doug.

"Juliette?"

She heard his silent fear, but he no longer needed to prove anything to her, and by trusting him without reading that article she hoped to prove that to him.

Besides, trusting Doug was easy because she'd learned to trust herself. "I already know I've got an intelligent man who puts me first."

Doug's heart filled with love and satisfaction—emotional satisfaction because he'd found his other half. A woman he loved to distraction who put her complete faith in him. He'd just have to make damn certain he never let her down.

"I promise to read the article," she said.

But her actions belied her words as she began an erotic swirling of her hips and arching of her back, tormenting his already hard body with an enticing invitation—one he planned to take her up on, and he met her with determined thrusts of his own.

Her lashes fluttered shut and purred. "Mmm. Guess I'll be reading it later."

"Much, much later," he muttered. Unable to withstand her teasing and needing to be inside her, he took charge, tossing the blanket onto the floor and lifting her until she could ease herself onto him, joining them together again.

This time, forever.

The Fantasy Continues:

INTIMATE FANTASY

By Julie Kenner
Available July 2001

Three sizzling love stories
by today's hottest writers
can be found in...

Midnight Fantasies....

Feel the heat!

Available July 2001

MYSTERY LOVER—*Vicki Lewis Thompson*

When an unexpected storm hits, rancher Jonas Garfield
takes cover in a nearby cave...and finds himself seduced
senseless by an enigmatic temptress who refuses to tell him
her name. All he knows is that this sexy woman wants him.
And for Jonas, that's enough—for now....

AFTER HOURS—*Stephanie Bond*

Michael Pierce has always considered costume shop
owner Rebecca Valentine no more than an associate—
until he drops by her shop one night and witnesses the
mousy wallflower's transformation into a seductive siren.
Suddenly he's desperate to know her much better.
But which woman is the real Rebecca?

SHOW AND TELL—*Kimberly Raye*

A naughty lingerie party. A forbidden fantasy. When Texas
bad boy Dallas Jericho finds a slip of paper left over from
the party, he is surprised—and aroused—to discover that he
is good girl Laney Merriweather's wildest fantasy. So what
can he do but show the lady what she's been missing....

*Harlequin truly does
make any time special....
This year we are celebrating
weddings in style!*

To help us celebrate, we want you to tell us how wearing the Harlequin wedding gown will make your wedding day special. As the grand prize, Harlequin will offer one lucky bride the chance to **"Walk Down the Aisle" in the Harlequin wedding gown!**

There's more...

For her honeymoon, she and her groom will spend five nights at the **Hyatt Regency Maui.** As part of this five-night honeymoon at the hotel renowned for its romantic attractions, the couple will enjoy a candlelit dinner for two in Swan Court, a sunset sail on the hotel's catamaran, and duet spa treatments.

A HYATT RESORT AND SPA   Maui • Molokai • Lanai

To enter, please write, in, 250 words or less, how wearing the Harlequin wedding gown will make your wedding day special. The entry will be judged based on its emotionally compelling nature, its originality and creativity, and its sincerity. This contest is open to Canadian and U.S. residents only and to those who are 18 years of age and older. There is no purchase necessary to enter. Void where prohibited. See further contest rules attached. Please send your entry to:

Walk Down the Aisle Contest

You can also enter by visiting www.eHarlequin.com
Win the Harlequin wedding gown and the vacation of a lifetime!
The deadline for entries is October 1, 2001.

HARLEQUIN®
Makes any time special®

PHWDACONT1

1. To enter, follow directions published in the offer to which you are responding. Contest begins April 2, 2001, and ends on October 1, 2001. Method of entry may vary. Mailed entries must be postmarked by October 1, 2001, and received by October 8, 2001.

2. Contest entry may be, at times, presented via the Internet, but will be restricted solely to residents of certain geographic areas that are disclosed on the Web site. To enter via the Internet, if permissible, access the Harlequin Web site (www.eHarlequin.com) and follow the directions displayed online. Online entries must be received by 11:59 p.m. E.S.T. on October 1, 2001.

   In lieu of submitting an entry online, enter by mail by hand-printing (or typing) on an 8½" x 11" plain piece of paper, your name, address (including zip code), Contest number/name and in 250 words or fewer, why winning a Harlequin wedding dress would make your wedding day special. Mail via first-class mail to: Harlequin Walk Down the Aisle Contest 1197, (in the U.S.) P.O. Box 9076, 3010 Walden Avenue, Buffalo, NY 14269-9076, (in Canada) P.O. Box 637, Fort Erie, Ontario L2A 5X3, Canada.

   Limit one entry per person, household address and e-mail address. Online and/or mailed entries received from persons residing in geographic areas in which Internet entry is not permissible will be disqualified.

3. Contests will be judged by a panel of members of the Harlequin editorial, marketing and public relations staff based on the following criteria:

   • Originality and Creativity—50%
   • Emotionally Compelling—25%
   • Sincerity—25%

   In the event of a tie, duplicate prizes will be awarded. Decisions of the judges are final.

4. All entries become the property of Torstar Corp. and will not be returned. No responsibility is assumed for lost, late, illegible, incomplete, inaccurate, nondelivered or misdirected mail or misdirected e-mail, for technical, hardware or software failures of any kind, lost or unavailable network connections, or failed, incomplete, garbled or delayed computer transmission or any human error which may occur in the receipt or processing of the entries in this Contest.

5. Contest open only to residents of the U.S. (except Puerto Rico) and Canada, who are 18 years of age or older, and is void wherever prohibited by law; all applicable laws and regulations apply. Any litigation within the Province of Quebec respecting the conduct or organization of a publicity contest may be submitted to the Régie des alcools, des courses et des jeux for a ruling. Any litigation respecting the awarding of a prize may be submitted to the Régie des alcools, des courses et des jeux only for the purpose of helping the parties reach a settlement. Employees and immediate family members of Torstar Corp. and D. L. Blair, Inc., their affiliates, subsidiaries and all other agencies, entities and persons connected with the use, marketing or conduct of this Contest are not eligible to enter. Taxes on prizes are the sole responsibility of winners. Acceptance of any prize offered constitutes permission to use winner's name, photograph or other likeness for the purposes of advertising, trade and promotion on behalf of Torstar Corp., its affiliates and subsidiaries without further compensation to the winner, unless prohibited by law.

6. Winners will be determined no later than November 15, 2001, and will be notified by mail. Winners will be required to sign and return an Affidavit of Eligibility form within 15 days after winner notification. Noncompliance within that time period may result in disqualification and an alternative winner may be selected. Winners of trip must execute a Release of Liability prior to ticketing and must possess required travel documents (e.g. passport, photo ID) where applicable. Trip must be completed by November 2002. No substitution of prize permitted by winner. Torstar Corp. and D. L. Blair, Inc., their parents, affiliates, and subsidiaries are not responsible for errors in printing or electronic presentation of Contest, entries and/or game pieces. In the event of printing or other errors which may result in unintended prize values or duplication of prizes, all affected game pieces or entries shall be null and void. If for any reason the Internet portion of the Contest is not capable of running as planned, including infection by computer virus, bugs, tampering, unauthorized intervention, fraud, technical failures, or any other causes beyond the control of Torstar Corp. which corrupt or affect the administration, secrecy, fairness, integrity or proper conduct of the Contest, Torstar Corp. reserves the right, at its sole discretion, to disqualify any individual who tampers with the entry process and to cancel, terminate, modify or suspend the Contest or the Internet portion thereof. In the event of a dispute regarding an online entry, the entry will be deemed submitted by the authorized holder of the e-mail account submitted at the time of entry. Authorized account holder is defined as the natural person who is assigned to an e-mail address by an Internet access provider, online service provider or other organization that is responsible for arranging e-mail address for the domain associated with the submitted e-mail address. **Purchase or acceptance of a product offer does not improve your chances of winning.**

7. Prizes: (1) Grand Prize—A Harlequin wedding dress (approximate retail value: $3,500) and a 5-night/6-day honeymoon trip to Maui, HI, including round-trip air transportation provided by Maui Visitors Bureau from Los Angeles International Airport (winner is responsible for transportation to and from Los Angeles International Airport) and a Harlequin Romance Package, including hotel accomodations (double occupancy) at the Hyatt Regency Maui Resort and Spa, dinner for (2) at Swan Court, a sunset sail on Kiele V and a spa treatment for the winner (approximate retail value: $4,000); (5) Five runner-up prizes of a $1000 gift certificate to selected retail outlets to be determined by Sponsor (retail value $1000 ea.). Prizes consist of only those items listed as part of the prize. Limit one prize per person. All prizes are valued in U.S. currency.

8. For a list of winners (available after December 17, 2001) send a self-addressed, stamped envelope to: Harlequin Walk Down the Aisle Contest 1197 Winners, P.O. Box 4200 Blair, NE 68009-4200 or you may access the www.eHarlequin.com Web site through January 15, 2002.

Contest sponsored by Torstar Corp., P.O. Box 9042, Buffalo, NY 14269-9042, U.S.A.

PHWDACONT2

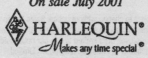

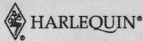

Fantasies Inc.

**An exclusive agency that caters to
intimate whims, provocative requests
and decadent desires...**

**Four lush island resorts waiting to
transport guests into a private world of
sensual adventures, erotic pleasures
and seductive passions...**

**A miniseries that will leave readers
breathless and yearning for more...**

Don't miss:
#832 _SEDUCTIVE FANTASY_ by Janelle Denison
Available May 2001

#836 _SECRET FANTASY_ by Carly Phillips
Available June 2001

#840 _INTIMATE FANTASY_ by Julie Kenner
Available July 2001

#844 _WILD FANTASY_ by Janelle Denison
Available August 2001

Do you _have_ a secret fantasy?

HARLEQUIN®

Temptation.